The Beasts of Belladonna

The Beasts of Belladonna

Stories

GILBERT ALLEN

THE BEASTS OF BELLADONNA
Stories

Copyright © 2020 Gilbert Allen. All rights reserved. Except for brief quotations in critical publications or reviews, no part of this book may be reproduced in any manner without prior written permission from the publisher. Write: Permissions, Wipf and Stock Publishers, 199 W. 8th Ave., Suite 3, Eugene, OR 97401.

Slant
An Imprint of Wipf and Stock Publishers
199 W. 8th Ave., Suite 3
Eugene, OR 97401

www.wipfandstock.com

HARDCOVER ISBN: 978-1-7252-6563-9
PAPERBACK ISBN: 978-1-7252-6564-6
EBOOK ISBN: 978-1-7252-6565-3

Cataloguing-in-Publication data:

Names: Allen, Gilbert.

Title: The beasts of belladonna : stories / Gilbert Allen.

Description: Eugene, OR: Slant, 2020

Identifiers: ISBN 978-1-7252-6563-9 (hardcover) | ISBN 978-1-7252-6564-6 (paperback) | ISBN 978-1-7252-6565-3 (ebook)

Subjects: LCSH: Short stories, American -- 21st century.| Short stories, American. | South Carolina -- Fiction. | Greenville County (S.C.) -- Fiction. | FICTION / Literary.

Classification: PS3551.L3923 B4 2020 (print) | PS3551.L3923 (ebook) |

Manufactured in the U.S.A.   October 5, 2020

For Barbara, the true *bella donna*

Allow not nature more than nature needs,
Man's life's as cheap as beast's.

—*King Lear*, II, iv

Contents

Prayers | 1

Fat Eyes | 10

Nobody Ever Looked Back on Life
and Wished for a Station Wagon | 20

Hospital Food | 33

Trash | 40

Standard Kung Fu Mayhem | 51

Inflatable Kids | 64

Weather | 71

Dog Days | 79

Treenapping | 87

Breaking News | 96

The Eye of the Needle | 101

Tails | 109

Confessions | 120

Gato | 134

Acknowledgments | 147

Prayers

I'LL BE HONEST WITH YOU: I didn't like the new preacher. For one thing, he looked like Liberace, all baby fat and jewelry beneath mounds of wavy dark hair that must have been dyed to match his clerical collar. I half expected his fingers to rattle when he jogged by the house and waved to me while I was still in my pajamas, taking out the kitchen garbage.

When my wife went into the hospital for her tonsillectomy, he was waiting for us after we'd gotten past Admitting. Don't ask me how he did it. We hadn't even known the room number ourselves until five minutes beforehand. He smiled and asked us if we'd been blessed by God. Since the doctors had told Hilda not to talk, it was up to me to supply the answer.

"We don't know," I said. "Perhaps you should come back this afternoon."

"Of course," he said, taking his clipboard from the metal sink by the door and scanning it quickly. He stuffed it under his arm and placed both hands squarely around Hilda's neck.

I'd already gotten out of my chair when he started praying.

"Dear God," he chanted, his own Adam's apple quivering as he raised his blue eyes to the suspended ceiling. "Dear God, please bless this throat and all that is inside it, so it may once again sing Your praises in Your own house." Hilda was lead soprano at Belladonna Methodist. "The music of Your name is great, and it is in that name and in the name of Your only Son and in the name of Your Holy Spirit that we pray. Amen."

I cleared my throat. After he'd left, Hilda went into the bathroom to put on her hospital gown. She came out with her dress folded into a perfect square and her teeth clenched, defining her jaw. She always puts on that expression when I'm angry for what she's convinced herself is no good reason. I laughed aloud. "Okay," I said. "Okay."

When she was back in bed, waiting for the nurse, and thought I'd forgotten all about Reverend Paulsen, I spoke in my most innocent voice. "Your Pastor-Parish Relations Committee really knows how to pick them, doesn't it?"

She took a small pad of paper from the nightstand and scribbled on it before she tossed it across the room.

SO HE'S A LITTLE FLAMBOYANT
TRY TO BE NICE TO HIM, YOU INFIDEL

And then she closed her eyes, but I could tell she was getting nervous. She hadn't been in the hospital since she was born.

§

I TRIED. I MET HIM again as I was kissing Hilda at the entrance to the OR suite. He'd tapped me on the shoulder while I was still bent over her gurney.

"How's she feeling?"

Hilda had asked for a double dose of valium, so at the moment she wasn't feeling much of anything. I don't think she knew that either of us were within twenty yards. "She's fine," I whispered, as the orderly wheeled her through the fire doors. "She appreciates your coming all the way from Belladonna to see her."

He waved his left hand in what I understood to be a self-deprecating gesture. But what I mainly noticed were his three rings—silver, ruby, and gold. His fingers seemed oddly thin, given the broadness of his face and shoulders. Yet you couldn't call him obese, not really. He put his hand over my clavicle and led me to the visitors' elevator.

We sat in the cafeteria over two cups of coffee for an hour and forty-five minutes. I tried every means I could think of to get rid of him—telling him that I knew *he* was a busy man, mentioning all the shut-ins and shaky marriages in his congregation that I could think of. But the more I spoke, the more he wanted to listen. For you see, Reverend Paulsen had just arrived in Belladonna Commons— our wannabe subdivision, just beyond the security gates of the *real*

Belladonna—on what Methodists call Relocation Day. Every minister in South Carolina has to be out of his old sinecure by 9:00 a.m. so his replacement can move in by noon. It's efficient, I'll give them that much.

The reverend said he'd recently "gone through" a divorce, so he appreciated any information about his flock that I could provide. I followed his logic well enough to realize I never wanted to come back as a minister's wife. I said, "You'll need to see Butler Breedlove about your complimentary renter's insurance."

"I surely could use another cup of coffee," he said. "Why don't you tell me a little something about yourself?"

By that time I had resigned myself to his company. "I'm a biology teacher."

"What exactly do you do?"

I was in the middle of my worst summer school class in recent memory. "Waste good frogs," I said. "Preserve the school district's microscopes."

His eyes drifted out the window. "My wife was a music teacher," he said. "I think she'll be going back to it in the fall." Now his eyes returned to me. "Bless her soul."

§

THE OPERATION WENT WELL. A couple of days later, while I was helping Hilda pack her things to go home, Reverend Paulsen walked by on his way to another room. I cursed myself for leaving that oversized door open, but my wife seemed genuinely glad to see him again—though she still couldn't talk. I snapped the latches of her suitcase with what I hoped was finality, but when I looked up he was holding Hilda's wrist with one hand and had the other one extended for me.

"Let us pray," he intoned.

I had no choice, and I suspected he knew it. When I grabbed his hand, he squeezed my fingers like he never meant to let them go. Half in surprise, half in anger, I squeezed back. Unfortunately, he took it as a gesture of spiritual solidarity. "Noel, could you offer a word of thanks for us?"

This time Hilda didn't dare look at my face. "Certainly," I said. "Dear God, preserve us from those who enter rooms without knocking. Save us from those who never pay for their own cups of coffee. And most of all, deliver us from those who would meddle in our private lives in Your name. Amen."

I dropped his hand and picked up the suitcase.

Unfortunately, the reverend had permission from the nursing staff to escort the wheelchairs of discharged patients. According to recent research, time seems to elongate by a factor of ten for those in acute physical or psychological distress. I can vouch for it. I thought that the elevator was going to Hell, not to the ground floor. Hilda's tears were streaming through her makeup; I'd have felt better if she'd kicked me in the groin. After I'd gotten her into our Toyota, Reverend Paulsen spoke softly to me from the curb. "I've already forgiven you, Noel. I just hope Jesus has."

§

Two weeks later, when my wife was speaking to me again, I drove her to her post-operative checkup. Everything was fine; she could start singing by the end of the month, just as long as she didn't overdo it. When we got back to Belladonna Commons, Hilda was visibly happier than she'd been since her last solo.

"By Christmas you should be one hundred percent," I said.

Tigger and Lambchop, our twin tabbies, were waiting for us. "Look at that," I said, trying to sustain my wife's good spirits. "We've got a welcoming committee!"

But they seemed uninterested in us. They were cackling at the front door, their front paws propped against the lower panels, their muzzles raised in what could have been supplication. Something had their undivided attention.

Hilda got out of the car and walked up the porch steps. "Oh my God," she said, covering her mouth.

Hilda's a little squeamish. After I ran up to see what had frightened her, my own stomach turned. A large robin had been nailed straight through the chest to the door's center panel, right below the peephole. Its wings and legs were splayed outward; its beak rested against the steel head. It didn't look like it had been dead very long.

Now Hilda was vomiting into the foundation plantings, and the cats were still at the door. Enraged, I stuck my fingers between the feathers and the oak panel, and pulled. When I threw the bird into the boxwoods, Tigger and Lambchop went into full gallop. Hilda had just finished retching, and she was trying to wipe off her mouth with a Kleenex.

Damn him, I thought. *Damn him.*

§

"You're crazy," she said that evening at the supper table.

"Don't ask me how, but I know he did it."

"I never told him about the doctor's appointment," she said. "How could he know we were *both* gone? Our truck was right in the driveway."

"He jogs by here every morning. He could've knocked to see if we were home."

"It was probably one of your juvenile delinquents," she said.

I hadn't thought of that. I'd just finished summer school that week, and I'd had to fail three kids who'd already flunked biology once. They were all basketball players, and though they needed the course to be academically eligible in the fall, they'd spent the whole summer playing tic-tac-toe in the wax at the bottom of the dissecting pans. I fingered the nail in my pocket, which I'd decided to keep. "Maybe you're right."

"Of course I am," she said.

§

But I had to find out for certain, so I devised a small experiment. One Sunday in September I asked Hilda if she thought the reverend might be looking for a jogging partner. She stared at me like I'd asked her to undress in the middle of our kitchen floor.

"I could stand to lose a few pounds," I said.

"Maybe you could." She tried not to smile as she buttered her morning muffin. "Would you like to come to church and ask him yourself?"

I didn't want to look too eager. That might have made both of them suspicious. "I was hoping you could ask him for me."

"Certainly," she said. "We'll let you know." And she was humming to herself in major keys for the rest of the day.

§

WE STARTED OUT SLOWLY, for my benefit—just a couple of miles every Wednesday afternoon. By Christmas we'd worked up to five miles three times a week. We didn't talk much at first, but as the days passed under our feet we chatted about the state lottery (he was for it), video poker (against), and the finer points of theology.

"There's something I've always wondered about," I said as we were both bent over, clutching our knees in the driveway, trying to catch our breaths. Tigger stopped rubbing against the rear tire of the reverend's Lumina as I lifted my shoulders and pointed upward. "Do animals have souls? Birds, for example."

If he felt uneasy, he didn't show it. "What makes you ask?"

"Just curious," I said, walking up to my own front door. "Ebenezer, would you take a look at this?" I had filled my voice with as much surprise as it would hold.

He strode from his car to join me. "Might be blood," he said. He took out a handkerchief and started rubbing the spot. "It's been there for quite a while, Noel."

Hilda would have to pick that moment to open the door. Ebenezer nearly fell into her arms over the threshold. "Would anyone like a cold drink?"

"Just water," the reverend said, tucking the handkerchief back into his sweat suit.

After she'd ushered him into the kitchen, she came back on the porch for me and closed the door. "I'm ashamed of you, Noel Willis," she hissed.

And, in truth, so was I.

§

ONE RAINY EVENING in March, the Belladonna Methodist Pastor-Parish Relations Committee decided that Reverend Paulsen would be better off with another congregation. "One a little less . . . sophisticated," she said wearily, hanging her dripping overcoat on the brass tree in the hallway. "And they think we need a minister with a wife. Two souls for the price of one, I guess."

I nearly choked on a taco chip, because Hilda doesn't have a cynical bone in her body. After I muted the college basketball game on the TV, I said, "How did you vote?"

"It was unanimous," she said, staring straight down at me. "Why should he have to put up with the crazies around here?"

"I've said I'm sorry, okay? What else do you want me to do?"

"There's nothing *to* do. He'll leave without knowing about your little experiment." I'd made the mistake of using that word back in December. "Let's not disillusion the poor man entirely."

§

EVENTUALLY, THOUGH, we did find something to do. In June we helped Ebenezer clean the parsonage on the day before he had to move out. For Hilda's sake, I insisted on doing all the messiest jobs—the bathrooms, the kitchen floor, the oven. Ebenezer had broiled a lot of hamburgers.

"You'd better wear rubber gloves for that," Ebenezer said.

But it wasn't any worse than the lab at school, and I told him so.

We didn't finish until midnight. On the way to the foyer we passed all of Ebenezer's possessions, boxed neatly on the floor. He'd probably be able to fit them into his minivan without having to use the rack up top. Ebenezer's materialism seemed limited to whatever he could wear on his fingers and around his neck at a given moment.

He took our hands and offered a prayer. Through an act of will, or perhaps faith, I listened to his voice but not to the words.

"That was beautiful," my wife murmured, dropping Ebenezer's hand but not my own.

"It was," I said, trying my best to mimic my wife's intonation. "Thank you."

§

EBENEZER ASKED ME for one last favor: to take his trash to the county dump after he'd left for Cowpens, his next ministerial appointment. He put his slender hand on my shoulder. "Nobody should begin his new life at Belladonna Methodist with garbage bags on his lawn."

I was glad we agreed on something.

School was already out—for once, I had no failures—so I was able to drive by at 9:30 a.m. to do my last bit of penance. There were five green sacks in a small circle by the sidewalk in front of what had been Ebenezer's home. As I was testing my lower back, I noticed something nestled between them. It was a battered birdcage, with a blue parakeet still inside it, alive, without food or water.

I felt vindicated. I put the bird on the passenger's seat of the truck and drove to Mall Mart. I bought a new cage, feeder cups, a water dispenser, a silver bell, and a cuttlebone. I kept the air conditioner running while I hauled the bags out to the landfill. I watched them go tumbling down the ledge, like lost souls, and I thought about Ebenezer.

When I got home, I gave the bird to Hilda and told her nothing about where I'd gotten it. Maybe she thought Mall Mart still sold parakeets. Anyhow, she didn't ask. My humiliation might have been public, but my triumph would be secret. She told me she'd always wanted a bird.

Tigger and Lambchop took so little interest in our new pet that I wondered aloud about letting it fly through the house.

"Let's not tempt fate," Hilda said.

So we never did.

§

NEXT CHRISTMAS we received a card from Ebenezer. The red envelope was addressed to both of us, in an elaborate cursive, with my name first. I wanted to see if his taste in stationery would be as outlandish as his rings or his prayers, but he'd been Hilda's minister, not mine. I waited for her to come back from the Econoclast and put the perishables away, and then I handed her the letter opener.

On the front of the card, a pelican was feeding its young with drops of blood from its own breast. I looked uneasily at the little blue bird in the gilded cage in the corner of the dining room. Hilda had named it Dovie. "What does it say?"

"*Even a Bird Can Save a Soul*," she said, wiping her eyes. Hilda can get pretty sentimental at times. "He wrote it himself. Bless his heart."

For a while, I was mute as Dovie. But I finally said I was surprised he'd had it in him—knowing that, whatever our mutual sins, I had spoken the truth.

Fat Eyes

AFTER HER DADDY PHONED from the hospital, Harriet couldn't look at the country-cured hams without crying. Since he weighed nearly as much as she did—300 pounds—the doctors had decided to keep Henry for "observation," even though his heart monitor was putting the timer for the new deep-fat fryer to shame. Then and there, Harriet promised to spend more time *observing* them both.

At one-thirty, when the lunch stampede had dwindled to a few strays grazing at the salad bar, she told Demarcus, the assistant manager of Karrie's Kountry Kookhouse, that she'd be taking her two-week vacation "starting right now." She'd look in on Henry during visiting hours, mornings and evenings, and use the rest of her time to get started on the PoundsAway Program. She'd seen it advertised on the placemats at the restaurant for the past month. RESULTS GUARANTEED! LOSE THE WEIGHT! WAIT TO PAY!

"Baby, you're not fat," Demarcus said. "You're just—*comfortable*."

"Not like you," she said. "I'm no La-Z-Boy."

Demarcus threw her grin right back at her. "I never had no chair in mind, Harriet." He patted the worn red vinyl of the empty booth. "More like a love seat."

How come the blackest men had the best teeth? She untied her apron and tossed it onto the Formica. "Dream on, honey." Too bad Demarcus was married.

§

POUNDSAWAY (Incorporated) stuck out in the new strip shopping mall on the east side of Belladonna Commons, sandwiched between a florist and a Sara Lee outlet store. The glass doors opened with the wink of an electric eye, just like at the Econoclast. Except for the Weigh Station with a digital scale, it was one big open room lined with mirrors that hung like icicles down to the gray industrial carpet.

They'd told her the details over the phone. You paid one dollar for every pound you lost until you hit your goal weight. Then you went on Maintenance for at least a year, and, for the incentive, paid a little extra for whatever you gained back. They took her Master-Card number and said that programs started on the hour, nine to five, Mondays through Saturdays.

Now it was almost five o'clock. About two dozen white women were hovering around the scale, most of them skinny as humming-birds, shivering in leotards. Harriet was glad she'd decided to wear a fleece warmup suit. It might have been the middle of March, but it still felt colder inside the building than in the parking lot.

She decided to approach the one woman dressed in something Harriet might have found in her own closet. The name tag said JOLENE. "Why are they all wearing bedroom slippers?" Harriet whispered.

"Maintenance girls. Gotta make their goal weight every week. Weigh over, pay over. Ten dollars a pound. Five dollars a shoe." Jolene's laugh sounded more like a sneeze. "You learn to choose your clothes real careful around here."

"Couldn't they bring a coat?"

"If it goes through the door, it goes on the scale. Corporate policy."

Harriet fingered the name tag on her own jacket.

"Oh, you did good for the first time, Sugar. It'll just add to your base weight. That way you'll have a few ounces to play with later on."

A buzzer sounded, and one of the mirrors on the far side of the room opened from the back. A tiny blond with a Mary Lou Retton haircut appeared in the shortest shorts Harriet had ever seen. Harriet stared at her thighs, then looked down at her own arms glumly. It was no contest.

"Hi. My name's Bambi, and I'll be y'all's Loss Facilitator for today." She adjusted the Wonderbra under her tank top, then blew her coach's whistle. "Time to get our meat on the hoof, ladies!"

The skinniest women began to line up in front of the scale. Harriet and Jolene fell in at the end, where they couldn't see what Bambi was doing.

"Excellent!" Bambi said. "Ladies, what do we say?"

"Aaaaah."

Harriet began to wonder if she should report her credit card stolen—as of yesterday. Then she looked at Jolene. She wasn't thin, but she didn't look fat either, at least not by Harriet's standards. "How much've you lost since you started?"

"Me? Two hundred and fifty pounds."

Harriet felt her heart flutter.

Jolene grimaced. "That's twenty-five pounds, ten times. I'm glad my husband can afford it."

The *oooohs* were leading the *aaaahs* by about three to one. Most of the Maintenance girls weren't making their goal weights. Bambi had to go to the Weigh Station desk for extra credit-card slips.

The line finally shrunk to Harriet. "First time?" Bambi said.

Harriet nodded as she placed her left foot on the scale, then slowly raised her right one to join it.

"Three-oh-four. Congratulations, Harriet!" Bambi handed her a white thirty-two-ounce plastic cup with a scarlet straw sticking out of the top. It said MOST AMBITIOUS LOSER in block letters. "Your personalized diet will arrive in the mail next week. Until then, just remember—water has no calories! Drink whenever you feel hungry!"

Bambi told the rest of the women to form a circle, then cartwheeled into the center. She stood on her hands while she spoke. "Now that I've got y'all's attention, today we're going to work on self-denial."

Jolene's knee nudged Harriet's. "Two face lifts and a BMW and she's an expert on self-denial. Wait'll you hear about how she lost seven pounds for her balance-beam dismount."

§

"PORTION CONTROL!" the backflipping Bambi continued. "That's the key to Lifestyle Management! Now I'll need a volunteer." She stuck her final landing, then stared squarely at Harriet. "Who's our resident expert on portions?"

Harriet felt like a horseshoe magnet surround by an army of compass needles.

"Well, I work in Karrie's Kountry Kookhouse. I make them up all the time."

"Excellent!" Bambi said. "We eat what we see. We become what we eat." She hooked Harriet by the elbow and hauled her to the nearest mirror. "We see what we become." Bambi faced the group and pointed her thumb backward over her shoulder. "Harriet is living proof."

Bambi took a Ziploc bag and a postal scale out of the Weigh Station desk drawer.

"Sliced turkey breast," Harriet said. "You'd better refrigerate that."

"It's for demonstration purposes," Bambi said. "Pure silicone. We won't be eating anything." Even when she frowned, the ends of her mouth still pointed upward. She handed Harriet the Ziploc bag but kept the small scale on her side of the Weigh Station. "Give me an ounce, Harriet. One ounce."

"I don't know if I can." Harriet felt herself blushing. She'd failed algebra in high school, twice. "I never was much good with numbers."

Bambi sighed. "Whatever you'd put on a sandwich."

Harriet took out the customary Karrie's portion for a Club Special, then lifted off one rubbery slice—then one more—to put back into the bag. "There," she said.

Her brown eyes dilating, Bambi walked backward to the mirrored door, then disappeared. She returned with somebody who looked like Dolly Parton before she hit puberty.

"What did I tell you, Melanie?"

Melanie's platinum hairdo moved slowly, from side to side. "Sweet Jesus, you're right! Those are the fattest eyes I've ever seen!"

Bambi dropped the loose silicone slices on the postal scale and waited for it to finish wobbling. "Four and a half ounces. What do we say, ladies?"

"Oooooh."

"See y'all next week," Bambi said.

Bambi stopped Harriet on her way out. "Maybe it's a perceptual problem. Maybe it has nothing to do with your character."

§

Harriet had planned to drive straight to the hospital, but now she decided to go to her daddy's empty house instead. Her mama drank herself to death in her wheelchair three years ago, in keeping with her conviction that women never had heart attacks—they were too busy giving them away. Harriet threw her MOST AMBITIOUS LOSER cup against the microwave oven. For the first time she could remember, Harriet envied Lucinda—all one hundred and thirty-three hillbilly pounds of her—safely underground, embalmed in her own Southern Comfort, where she couldn't cause any more damage.

Maybe her daddy hadn't done his laundry before feeling those chest pains on Thursday. Hopefully, Harriet checked the hamper in the bathroom—nothing, not even a pair of socks. So she walked back to the kitchen and looked for anything else that might require her attention. But the poor man had even emptied the dishwasher before driving himself to the hospital.

Her teeth had been clenched for the whole fifteen minutes since PoundsAway. They still were. She had to do *something*. So she gathered her daddy's clean shirts from the bedroom closet and carried them downstairs on their hangers. Ironing, she'd decided, might be even better than washing—for letting off steam.

The old ironing board stood next to the washer-dryer. When Harriet grabbed for the slender chain that had just brushed against her face, the overhead light didn't come on. She kept pulling and letting go, listening to it clicking, till she finally reached up to remove the bulb. But it was only loose in the socket, not burned out. After she turned it clockwise, it almost blinded her.

She looked down and rubbed the spots from her eyes. "First thing gone right today."

Trying not to smile, she smoothed the iron over the checkered cotton, enjoying the scent of the steam. It reminded her of cooking, without the calories. In twenty minutes she put her father's last shirt back on its hanger, admiring the crisp collar that would never come straight out of a dryer, no matter what the Permanent Press label said. She felt better. And she skipped supper for the first time she could remember.

§

FROM THE OPEN DOORWAY, he looked asleep. "Henry?" Ever since Harriet's mama had died, her daddy had insisted she call him by his first name. "How you feeling?"

"It's only 'cause I'm a veteran," he said, opening his eyes and waving his big right hand over the bedsheets. "That's why I'm still here. Frigging Commies."

Harriet grabbed his wrist to slow him down. She didn't want him pulling out his IV and making the machine next to his bed go crazy. "That's silly," she said.

"I got benefits, see? Good benefits. They know Uncle Sam gone take care of me, right down to the box he'll bury me in. If I was just Medicare, they'd've kicked my butt outta here this morning." He shoved the bed rail with his foot. "They know. Nurse even call me Sergeant."

Harriet smiled. Her daddy complained the way some people played five Bingo cards at once on Wednesday nights. "You still haven't told me how you're feeling."

"Like I got a sandbag on my chest." He snickered. "Taking a leak. I walked round the whole floor after lunch. Didn't even lean on the wall."

"Do tell."

"Last night they said my major arteries looked like LA during an earthquake. They didn't know I could hear." He shook his head. "I guess they need a laugh too. Job must get damn depressing. Dealing with fat niggers like me."

Harriet blushed for them both. Then she told him she'd started her program at PoundsAway. "Maybe you'd like to read these brochures," Harriet said, cautiously putting them under the case for his reading glasses. "They make a lot of sense, Henry."

"*Snacking on the Hoof. Feeding Your Guilt. Drowning Your Fat.* Read this? My goldfish are dying, and I'm supposed to worry 'bout drowning my fat?"

"I fed them," Harriet said. "Just came from the house."

"Bless you," he said. "Have a cheeseburger for me. They're in the freezer."

"Which one?" She wasn't planning to eat it, but at least she could throw it out to make him feel better.

"Upstairs. Cheeseburgers in Paradise. I only keep the stuff from the hunting trips downstairs." He gave her his best laugh of the day. "Went through Hell to get it. Figure it should stay there."

§

FOR THE NEXT WEEK, Harriet kept her water cup in plain sight, vacuumed the carpets three times a day (for the exercise), and slept over at her daddy's house. She stayed in her own bedroom—the one she couldn't remember ever *not* knowing, though the family had moved in when she was two and a half, almost thirty-five years ago. The bed hadn't seemed so small then. It held the whole world—her Barbies, her Kens, her stuffed Bullwinkle, even her best friend, Mary. A sweet, gap-toothed white girl who'd sneak inside and use the mattress as a trampoline whenever both their mamas were drunk, which was most every day.

Harriet bit her lip. Whenever she filled her big cup at the Frigidaire, she'd opened the freezer side and stared at the cheeseburgers, individually wrapped, stacked like old 45s in a jukebox. She'd stick the straw between her teeth and suck deeply. *Portion Control. We eat what we see.* Today, she shut her eyes and closed the skinny door. She'd have to weigh in again the day after tomorrow.

She sucked more water, then sniffed suspiciously. Something seemed to float over the potpourri that she'd put on the kitchen table. She inspected the vegetable bins and found two withered apples and a soft potato with a black bottom. She double-wrapped them in plastic grocery bags and threw them into the garbage pail.

When she came back from her morning visit to the hospital, the smell was still there—only more so. She checked the bags—they didn't seem to be leaking. Squatting on her knees in the dining room, she sniffed the carpet. The scent was stronger but coming from no place in particular. Maybe your sense of smell got better when you ate less. She'd already cracked 300 naked pounds on Henry's bathroom scale.

She decided that putting Lysol into the toilets and sinks might help. Her daddy stored all the cleaning supplies downstairs, so she trudged down the hallway.

When she opened the door to the basement, she gagged.

The stairwell light flickered and popped, so she had to step slowly in darkness, holding her breath, listening to the wooden stairs creaking beneath her.

Groping her way to the laundry room, she could feel her feet sticking to the concrete. She breathed through her mouth as shallowly as she could. When she pulled the light chain, the bulb dimmed and wavered as soon as it went on. A soft whirring began from the concrete wall behind her.

In daylight the dark puddles might have been brown or red. The biggest one sat at the bottom of the freezer. She opened the door—then kicked it shut, coughing, leaving a bloody footprint under the handle.

This is what we eat. This is what we become.

§

"Calm down, Harriet. Come on girl, just spit it out."

She stammered about the stench, the blood, the soggy mess still in the freezer.

"You downstairs before?"

She sniffled. "I ironed your shirts last week."

"Did you turn off the light? With the chain?"

She nodded.

"It's the only good socket in the basement now. That's why I loosen the bulb. So the freezer keep running."

She knelt on the linoleum squares and put her head on the bedsheets, sobbing. "I'm sorry, Daddy. I'm so sorry."

"Hey there," he said, patting the crown of her head. "It's just an old deer I shot three years ago. Could have died a natural death by now."

"The smell," Harriet said. "You can't imagine it."

"Just throw everything into some Heftys and hose down the floor. Use the Wet Vac to suck it up."

"Can I put some bleach in the water?"

"Sure, honey. Much as you want." He lifted her chin with the tip of his finger. "OK?"

She could still feel her own shoulders shaking. "The body, Henry," she said. "Where should I bury it?"

"The trash, honey. Put it in the trash."

"Mister Pritchard won't take it. It's disgusting, it's—oh God, those white women stare at me like I'm some kind of animal."

Now he held her face in both his hands. "You my baby," he said. She could still see the scab from his IV line. "Did I ever tell you you got named after me?"

"After you?"

"That's right. Henry. Harry. Harriet. Lucinda and me—well, we didn't always fight. That was just her pain speaking. We got along good, before she messed up her back. You should've seen her. Anyway, we *sure* you gone be a boy. Don't ask me how. And she wanted to name you after me. She insisted. And you know how your mama got when she insisted on anything."

"God yes," Harriet said.

"So you were little Henry for six months. Boy, were we surprised."

She was still crying, but she laughed anyway. "You mean *girl*."

"Harriet was my idea." He wiped her cheek with the corner of his bedsheet. "After a few weeks, we wondered why we ever wanted a boy. You should've seen the look in your mama's eye whenever she fed you." He smiled. "Things got a way of working out. Just stay away from those skinny little bitches." He picked up *Drowning Your Fat* from the nightstand and Frisbeed it through the open doorway of the bathroom. "Did I hit the toilet for once?"

"Almost," she laughed. "Almost, Henry."

§

HARRIET COULDN'T EVEN think about sleeping until she'd cleaned up the basement. She found a dust mask next to the paint brushes, which cut the stench if she kept her breaths short and shallow.

It took her till four o'clock in the morning, and she felt proud of herself. Mister Pritchard, if he was on time for once in his life, would be coming at dawn—she hadn't wanted the neighborhood dogs and cats to be tempted for a whole week before the next pickup. And after the bleach and the Wet Vac, the basement smelled more like a swimming pool than a slaughterhouse.

Now it didn't seem worth going to sleep. She had her instant coffee—no sugar, no cream, plenty of hot water—and waited for the garbage truck to make its morning rounds.

Then she decided to weigh in a day early.

She took a Ziploc bag from the kitchen cabinet and walked outside to the curb.

She held her breath and untwisted the plastic tie on the black Hefty. Then she took out the first piece she could find—a shoulder roast still dripping in Handi-Wrap—and shoved it inside the clear one-gallon bag.

Inside her father's house, Harriet ran her fingernail along the raised seam, just to make sure it was perfect. *Doe, a deer, a female deer . . . .* Let's see her slice off an ounce from *this*. And when doe-eyed Bambi tells her it stinks, it's disgraceful, it's disgusting, she'll just *oooooh* and tell her to have a little more respect—for her relations.

Nobody Ever Looked Back on Life and Wished for a Station Wagon

THEY WERE ALONE IN THE first row of Kiddie Klassik Kartoons, watching *The Lion King*. Marjorie Breedlove was yawning at swirling ostriches, orbiting giraffes, kaleidoscopic zebras, and thinking *Fantasia in Africa* . . . . Then the child's fingers were tapping the back of her hand. She leaned her head toward Angela and felt a moist whisper in her ear.

"The next scene is *very* intense. It is not suitable for *all* viewers. You *may* want to close your eyes."

But Marjorie's eyes were already closed, so she opened them.

The scruffy little cub—she'd forgotten his name—was clinging to the horizontal branch of a dead tree, suspended over a stampede of what? Horses? Did Africa have horses? Then the dust became her own driveway, the hooves the pistons of one engine, *her* engine, a roar of impatience, *her* impatience, and she thought *Pinky*.

Angela stood up, backlighted by the giant screen, her first-grader's face a featureless shadow. She pointed her tiny flashlight between Marjorie's eyes.

"Just what I thought." She tugged at Marjorie's wrist, her whisper becoming more urgent. "If you cry, Mrs. Breedlove, you come with me to the lobby. Your movie is *over*."

Marjorie stood, grabbing the straps of her pocketbook with her free hand. She watched the flashlight's thin beam sweep over the empty seats, toward the carpeted aisle.

"I'm sorry," Angela said. "But those are the rules."

§

HER HUSBAND HAD brought the child home that morning, while she was clearing dead flowers from Pinky's grave. She'd just gone outside, after the sun had managed to soften the first hard frost of the season. It had come late, the Saturday after Thanksgiving.

The little girl clutched a pink vinyl suitcase in the hand that Butler wasn't holding. "This is Angela," he proclaimed. "Angela, this is Mrs. Breedlove."

Marjorie pulled off her stained gloves and dropped them into the wheelbarrow. She had to squint at Angela, who was wearing a white jumper that reflected the low winter light. Its hem nearly touched the withered grass. "Don't *you* look ready to travel," Marjorie said.

"Not me. My mommy and daddy."

"Bambi and Mike," Butler said. "It's their anniversary. So Angela will be staying with us."

"Of course." Marjorie stretched her lips into a smile. "Might I ask for how long?"

Angela had left her suitcase on the patio and walked to the loosened black earth around Pinky's grave. She poked at the rectangular marker, tentatively, with the tip of her sneaker. Shaking her head, Marjorie grabbed the wooden handles of the wheelbarrow and started pushing it toward the compost heap at the edge of the vegetable garden.

When she arrived at her destination, Butler's voice came from behind her. "A week."

She shoved the handles from underneath until the wheelbarrow reeled over, upside down, the tire still spinning like an outtake from an action-adventure movie. "A *week*? And you didn't tell me?"

"I didn't know until yesterday. Yesterday afternoon. Mike's mother was going to take her, but she got the flu. And they've got non-refundable tickets to Bermuda."

"How convenient."

"And I guess I feel, well—*responsible* for Angela. You know?"

Marjorie tried to keep out of her husband's business, but she knew this particular story. Mike had come to Breedlove Insurance as a single father. When Butler hired Bambi a couple of years later, he'd assigned Mike as her mentor. In three months the tiny balance-beam gymnast had risen to Top Gun on the agency bulletin board—with an engagement ring on her celebratory photo. "Well, I'm glad you feel responsible for something."

He righted the wheelbarrow, then reached into the pile of withered petunias and sweet alyssum. He shook the blackened leaves from the gloves and handed them back to Marjorie, but his eyes were focused glumly upon their house. "I try."

It was true. He tried. When he'd put up those storm windows and ruined her flowers in the bargain, he'd replaced every one of them. Every one. And then he'd brought her Pinky.

"They're two of my best people, Marjorie. And just look at her." He pointed his thumb across the backyard.

With her index finger, Angela was slowly tracing the engraved letters on the polished granite.

"She's adorable," Marjorie admitted.

"I've already childproofed the guest room," her husband said, taking her hand, leading her back to the patio. "Marjorie, I owe you one on this."

She laughed. "I'll put that on my kitchen calendar."

After he'd carried the tiny suitcase inside, he said, "Somebody needs a ride to the airport. I'll let you two get acquainted. Okie-dokie?" Then he nearly sprinted to the car.

When they were standing alone on the patio, Angela's eyes rose to Marjorie's. "What's okie-dokie?"

The child was shivering. Marjorie checked her own hands—they were clean—then rested them on Angela's shoulders. "Baby, shouldn't you be wearing a jacket? It's almost December."

"Who's Pinky?"

"My cat," Marjorie said. "He died last March."

Angela's eyes widened. "How?"

"He was old." It was what she'd told everyone, even Butler.

"How old?"

"Thirteen." That, at least, was true. Butler had seen him sitting on the road's shoulder, staring fearlessly at the oncoming traffic, while they were driving home from the hospital after her last surgery. He'd stopped the Camry, picked the cat up, and carried him to the passenger's side, into her open hands. He was so tiny, and his nose so like the color of her own fingernails, that she'd named him in an instant. The next day, she was shocked when the vet told them he was probably ten years old. Butler insisted on plastering LOST CAT flyers with Pinky's picture all over the neighborhood, but thankfully no one had claimed him.

"That's old." Angela walked around the gravestone before she spoke again. "When are you going to dig him up?"

Marjorie's stomach could have been full of broken glass. "What do you mean?"

"Why did you put him down there?"

Marjorie closed her eyes. "Baby girl, have you had lunch?"

"I'm not hungry, thank you. My new mommy made me a nutritious breakfast."

"Would you like to go—somewhere? To do something? To see a movie?"

"*The Lion King*!" Angela smiled the perfect, miniature smile that Marjorie knew she'd lose next year, sometime in the second grade. "I'll get the video for Christmas. If I'm good."

"I'll bet you're always good."

Inside, they checked the newspaper together, then left for the early matinee as soon as Angela found her jacket and her pocket flashlight. "Kiddie Klassik Kartoons," Angela explained, "does *not* have adequate lighting."

§

PINKY DIED ON A COLD Monday morning, after Marjorie had returned from her weekly safari to the Econoclast. She'd hauled in all the plastic bags, held her bladder until she'd unpacked and refrigerated the perishables—and then couldn't find a bathroom with toilet paper. She'd sworn at herself, used some of the facial tissues from the box on top of the tank, and sprinted back to the Camry. She'd be hosting the Greater Belladonna Garden Club at eleven-thirty, and some of those women were like watering cans that had never made it past Quality Control .

When she turned the key, for less than a heartbeat her engine strained—so she stamped her right foot till it roared. She watched her rear view mirror, careful to avoid the wheelbarrow she'd left in the turnaround. It could wait till she got home.

Twenty minutes later, gunning her car up the driveway, she saw a dark stain that began in front of the garage. It led to the back door, where she found Pinky, twisted across the word WELCOME. Warm. Dead.

At first she'd thought the new collie from across the street had mauled him. She'd prepared herself for this. Pinky loved to be outdoors, and Marjorie knew that he'd rather take his chances with the neighborhood dogs than give up his freedom. Then she remembered that the stain began where she usually parked her car.

She dropped her purse, ran back to check all her tires. She thanked God they were clean. But the blotch wasn't where her tires would have been. It was more in the center of the driveway. Under her hood.

Her hands shook as she fingered the latch above the front bumper. Blood flecked the TOYOTA logo on the engine. Bits of flesh and white fur were still clinging to the alternator belt.

She let the hood drop with its own weight.

It was a raw, cloudy day. There was no sun to sleep in, so he'd gone to the warmest place in the yard. He must have felt safe. It was, after all, her car.

She parked the Camry at the bottom of the driveway, with CANCELED in block letters soaped on the windshield.

The first day, the first week, the first month, she couldn't cry. But she could work. The wheelbarrow's tire had gone flat, so she'd inflated it with the bicycle pump she found in the garage, behind the emergency bag of Fresh Step. She'd wrapped Pinky in his bed—her old chenille bathrobe—and buried him in the back yard, at the bottom of the deepest hole she'd ever dug by herself. After she'd had the headstone engraved, after she'd spent the whole spring planting flowers, the whole summer watering them—then, finally, she cried. All September her sobs would come upon her like a thunderstorm, with about as much warning. At the premonitory tremble she'd hide in the hall closet, so Butler couldn't see her, and muffle her mouth with her sleeve.

Of course, she'd told the girl nothing of this. How could a six-year-old understand how guilt devoured mere logic? How her heart despised that part of herself which insisted, calmly and rationally, that the world was full of griefs so much greater than her own?

§

HER HUSBAND TOOK ANGELA to school on Monday. Marjorie had stayed in bed, her eyes fixed on the motionless ceiling fan, until she heard his Grand Prix slip into gear and shudder down the driveway.

Butler had left the morning paper on the kitchen table. She dawdled over the Cryptoquote till ten o'clock, when she knew her father would be claiming his free Senior Coffee at Hardee's. Then her fingers pressed her parents' number into the Touch Tone pad on the wall phone.

For years, Marjorie had communicated with her mother mainly by coupon. She'd write a perfunctory letter that her father would read—he opened every envelope that entered the house—and put her real letter deep inside a sheaf of SmartSaver clippings bunched together by a rubber band. Her father didn't believe in coupons. "Nickels and dimes," he'd sneer. But lately her mother hadn't been writing back, and during her monthly visits Marjorie had noticed a widening vacancy in her eyes and words.

On the third ring, her father answered, and Marjorie stifled a groan. He told her her mother was in a motel. Last week he'd tried to have the oil furnace serviced, but none of the repairmen would come to the house—*his* house—on a half-hour's notice. So he'd lugged the vacuum cleaner down the cellar stairs and done the job himself.

"I was watching the *front* of the damn thing." His New Jersey accent sounded even more earsplitting over the phone. "Who thinks of looking at the butt end of a vacuum cleaner?"

Apparently the whole place was now slathered with a layer of oily soot. He'd told the State Farm agent that the furnace had malfunctioned when he'd turned it on. "Blowback," he snorted. "Happens all the time. The adjuster came out and offered me five grand, right on the spot!" When her father laughed, he sounded like a hyena with a learning disability. "I think the guy ruined his suit when he sat on the sofa." He laughed again. "You know your Mom. She won't come back till she can eat offa the floor. I hired this kid from the carwash to do the furniture and the carpets. I'm gonna do the walls myself."

Marjorie stared at her kitchen ceiling.

"Dad's gonna come outta this with three grand up his wazzoo. Even with the deductible! By Christmas, Dad's gonna be smelling like a rose."

"Great for Dad," Marjorie muttered, but he didn't hear her. As usual. So she half-shouted, "What motel is Mom in?"

"One of them gyp joints off the highway. She called a cab. Why don't *you* call more often, honey? What news you got for Dad?"

"Not much. I cleared off the garden on Friday."

"Not your job," he declared. "Tell that husband of yours to get on the stick. Make Dad a grandpa already."

Marjorie put the receiver on the kitchen counter. She wasn't about to remind her own father she was forty-five years old.

"Dad's waiting."

She stared at the twisted, dangling cord in front of her own body. After she'd been diagnosed with distal tubal blockage, she'd asked her first surgeon how it happened—she'd never slept around, not even in college. "No way of telling," he said. "Maybe a secondary infection that didn't get treated." He looked up from her unsigned consent form. "Ever have a bad cold for more than a week?" And her mind had flown back to a December filled with her mother's whispering, while her father swore he wouldn't pour his good money into some doctor's Cadillac for a kid's sniffle. He'd blustered something about young bodies healing themselves. Always had, and always would. On New Year's Day, her first afternoon out of bed, he'd brought her to Howard Johnson for an ice-cream cone. Butter pecan. Two scoops.

"Cat got your tongue, honey?"

She raised the receiver from the countertop and dropped it on the hook. If he called back, she'd just let it ring.

§

On the Watchman wedged between Marjorie's cookbooks, Martha Stewart was doing Christmas decorations. She was in the middle of a mouse you could make out of a dried teasel, two pieces of pinecone, and three straight pins. When you finished, you could either nestle it right in the tree or hang it from a bent paper clip. Marjorie turned up the sound and got out her pencil and pad, just in case she ever went back to substitute teaching at Belladonna Elementary.

At the commercial break, she saw a car—a convertible the very color of her own Camry—driven by a blond whose hair stretched impossibly backward, like unearthly wings. The woman turned to the camera and smirked without opening her mouth. *Nobody*, her voice-over declaimed, *ever looked back on life and wished for a station wagon.*

"How do you know?" Marjorie threw her notepad at the tiny glowing screen. "Are you J.D. Power? Did you take a fucking *survey?*"

§

She told Butler she was having trouble sleeping, and she hauled her pillow into her study on the opposite end of the house. It had a convertible sofa. Butler knew he snored and gurgled intermittently, like a leaking toilet. She'd go back to the master bedroom just as soon as her body clock reset and she was no longer The Princess and the Pea. They'd been through this before, a dozen times.

The moment she had the kitchen to herself each morning, she'd start making dinner. Pasta Primavera. Poulet Marengo. Boeuf Bourguignon. Each evening, she'd say that she'd already eaten, serve Angela, then Butler, with a smile and a flourish, and start soaking the pots and pans in the sink. They were fast eaters. After she'd cleared the table, she pecked their cheeks in the family room, handed Butler the TV remote, and left to get her bed ready for the night. Angela's room was across the hall. She was, thank God, a quiet child.

But on Friday evening, after Marjorie had flossed her teeth and propped herself into her pillow with the latest issue of *Cooking Light*, she heard a soft knock. She stared at the silent door. When the knock came again, she knew the hand making it was no higher than the brass knob.

"Just a minute, baby girl." Her robe was draped over an Allied Van Lines carton filled with old lesson plans, and she pulled it over her shoulders. Then she released the lock button on the knob slowly, so it wouldn't click.

Angela was staring at her own slippers. White slippers. She was holding her flashlight in front of her lowered face. "Here," she said. "I'm not supposed to have this when I go to bed."

"Angela, I don't—"

"Tell them I gave it to you. Every night. Okie-dokie?"

Marjorie put the flashlight on top of a bookcase and smoothed Angela's hair. When she came to the little flip above the child's neck, she started to tickle her behind the ears. Mortified, she pulled her hand away and clutched the belt of her own bathrobe. "Okie-dokie." After the child left, Marjorie didn't close the door.

§

IT WASN'T LOUD. Not a scream or a sob—more like a moan that you'd make with your mouth closed. For how long? Marjorie shoved her hands against the thin mattress and stood up in the dark.

When she got to the guest room, she sat at the foot of the giant bed and whispered the child's name. But Angela kept moaning, out of reach.

Marjorie's fingers were fumbling for the wall switch when she remembered the overhead fixture would blind them both. So she went back to her study and returned with the flashlight. Marjorie opened the child's fingers and pressed the chrome handle into her hand.

"It's dark down there," Angela whispered. "It's so dark."

"I know, baby girl." Marjorie was kneeling at the side of the bed where Angela lay, twisted up in the sheets, pointing the tiny light down the vast mattress, toward the footboard.

"Pinky must be so afraid."

She managed to get back into the hallway before she bit the sleeve of her nightgown, to hold onto her own tears. Then she picked up her pillow and walked across the house to her own room, her own bed, her own husband, her own raveling dreams.

§

BUTLER HAD ALREADY taken Angela to Skateland for the day. He'd pulled a Post-it from her big pad and stuck it on the bathroom mirror. *Thanks for tucking us in.*

She found the flashlight back on the bookcase in her study. The batteries? Dead. So she jammed her legs into some old jeans and pulled a T-shirt down over the empty belt loops. She'd be going to the Econoclast.

When she looked at the digital clock glowing on the Camry's dashboard—11:15—she swung the steering wheel into a sudden left turn. She'd head for Mall Mart instead. She'd be needing more than just batteries.

§

SINCE THEIR PLANE was overbooked, and since they'd volunteered for an earlier flight—sweetened with a hefty voucher for their next vacation—Bambi and Mike had decided to splurge for a cab. Or so they'd explained, after Marjorie met them at the front door. They'd rung the bell, again and again, while she was still putting her Dustbuster back into the hall closet.

"Where's Butler?" Bambi finally said.

"He's with Angela. Roller skating. They should be back any minute." Marjorie led them into the living room and asked if they'd like something to drink.

"Something hot," Bambi said, rubbing her hands together, as if she were hoping they'd catch fire.

Marjorie left a samovar of coffee on a trivet before she excused herself to get Angela's things. Bambi had assumed they'd already been packed the night before, according to her instructions. Dresses, socks, jeans, T-shirts, panties—everything was white, except for the pink vinyl suitcase. Marjorie tried to fold the clothes the way a six-year-old might, unsure of the seams and creases, and brought the suitcase out to the foyer. Back in the living room, after lying about using her own toilet, Marjorie asked about Bermuda.

"Scooters," Mike said. "That's how everybody gets around over there. No bikes, no cars—just these little motor scooters."

"I have no earthly idea how the palmettos can stand it. We had to buy sweaters," Bambi said, pouting at her fuzzy blue sleeves. "You couldn't keep warm."

Mike grinned broadly. "I beg to differ."

Bambi refilled her own cup and wrapped her fingers around it. "We should've gone to St. Thomas."

"The Virgin Islands? On a *second* honeymoon?" Mike shook his head. "Bambi, give me a break."

"Men have no imagination." She winked at Marjorie. "And women have too much."

Marjorie smiled. "So what do you imagine?"

"At the moment?" Bambi sipped her black coffee. "Customer service on Monday morning, starting at eight o'clock. A whole week playing catch-up." She winced at her husband. "*After* I get your daughter ready for school."

"Hey, I make the oatmeal. I drive the van."

"Her wardrobe's nice and simple," Marjorie said.

"You know when to wash it," Bambi said. "It's like a good major medical plan. No surprises. White doesn't lie."

"I hope Angela wasn't too much trouble," Mike said.

"Not at all," Marjorie said, fixing her eyes upon Bambi's blue sweater.

"I envy you, Marjorie." She gestured toward the trackless green carpet. "Having the time for all this."

"Quality time," Mike said.

"Exactly," Bambi said. "Quality time. With no distractions."

They didn't hear Butler and Angela until they'd walked into the living room.

"Y'all found us." Bambi clapped her hands. "Good work."

"Marjorie, this girl can really skate. She's a natural."

"Lessons," Bambi said.

Butler hoisted the child onto her father's lap. "It shows."

Angela looked over the samovar at her new mother. "I saw the movie again."

Bambi shook her head. "That kiddie palace has been running it forever and a day." She helped herself to more coffee. "You'd think she'd get tired of watching those big old cats." Now she smiled at the child. "Were you a little baby?"

"Bambi," Mike said.

"But I didn't, Daddy! I didn't cry."

Butler shrugged his shoulders.

"She didn't," Marjorie said. "And I have a surprise for you, young lady. Right down the hall."

"Please Mommy?" Angela's two feet struck the carpet at the same time. "*Hakuna Matata?*"

"Mass marketing." Bambi sighed. "You try your level best to protect them, but you just can't."

In her storage room, Marjorie handed the child a small plastic bag.

"Batteries!"

"But here's the real surprise." Marjorie helped her slip the KiddyKat watch over her wrist. "You wear this to bed, young lady. And whenever you want, you just press the button and look at his face. Okie-dokie?"

"Okie-dokie," Angela said. "But what about Pinky?"

Marjorie forced herself to say his name.

"You still haven't helped *him*. I checked."

"I can't help him now. I wish I could." Marjorie wanted to stop herself, but her voice kept going. "And I didn't tell you the truth. Pinky was old. But that's not why he died."

"What did he do?"

"He had an accident, Angela. With a car. My car. He needs—we need you to know that."

"I could tell him," Angela said.

So she took the child into the garage, where she kept the white paper sacks and the luminary candles that would line their driveway for the neighborhood drop-in on Christmas Eve. "You take these," Marjorie said. "And your flashlight. I'll meet you in the back yard."

On the shelf at the right of the circuit breakers, Marjorie found some fireplace matches next to the hurricane lamp. She put them into her pocket, then grabbed the leftover bag of cat litter that still sat on the garage floor.

Outside, they took turns, half-filling the sacks with the dusty gravel, so they wouldn't blow away. Then Angela cradled the small candles in her hands, one by one, and lowered them into position. Marjorie struck the long match, and a wick soon flickered in every sack.

"Look," Angela said, her voice rising into the wind. "They're working."

They sat on the new pine straw together, their backs against Pinky's grave. And when they finally heard voices from outside their circle—dark voices, familiar voices—they were ready to go home.

Hospital Food

YOU REALLY WANT TO SIT HERE, lady? Then let me tell you something. Cosmic Truth. The universe is filled with possums, but all of them are dead. Believe me. I've looked. Eleven years with the highway department and I've never found one that wasn't Hamburger Helper. And you know how many other Cosmic Truths I've found stuck to the pavement? One. *Eins. Uno.* But he was a possum, too. Maybe you'd better write this down.

It ain't done it.

You got that? You're hearing this from the Henry Hudson of the Highway. The Balboa of the Blacktop. The Columbus of Concrete. I boldly go where no van has gone before. Drive my pickup all over Greenville County and phone in the potholes. I see each road once, maybe twice a month. Tell the DOT maintenance crews how much asphalt patch they'll need.

And to squeeze a little more blood out of your money—you pay taxes, don't you?—I scrape up the roadkill and throw it in the back of my truck. That's really how I spend most of my time. I've stopwatched it. My ratio's about three to one, carcasses to cavities.

They used to call me a Maintenance Locator. But by the end of last year, I'd had it. A decade with the same job description, and it's not even half right. I mean, I have aspirations. I'm human. I have two years of college. So I walk into Pendergast's office and tell him I want a new title. He doesn't even take his eyes off the computer screen. Virtual Zombie. "What?" he says. He's playing Minesweeper in the Words for Windows program.

I grab his mouse and say, "*No mas.* From now on, I'm a Pavement Imperfection Coordinator." The way I see it, potholes and possums both qualify as departures from the ideal. And I don't leave his office until he brings up my personnel file on his screen and changes my permanent record.

I should've stood up to him before. I've got some dignity. I don't do driveways. Sometimes people see my pickup with the Greenville County logo on the doors and flag me down to haul some dead Pomeranian off their property. Or some half-rotten raccoon from their crawl space. They think I'm the undertaker for the animal shelter. They tell me they pay their taxes and never see them again. I tell them *I* pay my taxes too, and if a dog drops dead in *my* yard, I leave it there. At least till I'm off my shift.

The Cosmic Truth? Couple of months ago, I'm standing on the shoulder of Pineforest Drive, prying this baby possum off the asphalt with my Removall. Precision instrument. Looks like a snow shovel, wide and with a big flange in the back. But it's steel instead of aluminum so it won't bend. Anyway, while I'm pallbearing the little sucker back to my truck, I hear this voice coming out of the sky. Like God, you know?

"It ain't done it."

I figure God has better grammar than that, so I look straight up. There's somebody with a chain saw about thirty feet off the ground. He's just standing there, held up by his spiked boots and his big leather belt wrapped around the tree.

"What?" I yell.

The tobacco juice lands smack on my shovel.

"It done tried to cross the road, but Melvin Wood seen when it ain't done it."

I toss the possum over the lip of my tailgate. "Thanks for—" But Melvin Wood fires up the saw and starts cutting off all the branches that're too close to the power lines. I get back in the truck before I get hit with something. I don't wear a helmet. It gives me a rash.

That afternoon, I'm driving the switchbacks all over the northern end of the county, and I can't get Melvin Wood's words out of my mind. *It ain't done it.* By Friday I figure out it's not just *an* answer, it's *the* answer. The Mother of All Answers. Why is every possum in the visible world dead? It ain't done it. Why is God invisible to modern theology? It ain't done it. Why does my marriage look like it's been run over by an eighteen-wheeler? It ain't done it. Why do I want to emasculate John Tesh?

It ain't done it.

My work began to take on a spiritual aspect. It didn't seem right, just sticking my Removall under those busted rumps and flinging them into the truck. Without using my own mouth to give some last morsel of meaning to their miserable little lives. No, I wasn't about to start eating them. I'm not that hungry. But I started keeping a copy of *Bartlett's Familiar Quotations* on my floor mat, on the passenger's side. One Hundred And Twenty-Fifth Anniversary Edition. Newly Enlarged. And I tried to look up something each time some poor *It ain't done it*.

Couple more weeks, and I've got a routine. I like to start off with a little Shakespeare, especially for a dog or a cat. *Love is not love*—scrape—*which alters when it alteration finds, or bends with the remover*—fling—*to remove*. Plop. Then it's back in the cab. The next one's usually a possum. *Beauty is a pledge of the possible conformity between the soul*—scrape—*and nature*. Fling. George Santayana. Plop. I always think of Susan when I say that one. *The art of being wise is the art of knowing what to overlook*. I usually save this for the Saint Bernards and the Great Danes I shove to the side of the road. I don't need another hernia. My insurance only paid for eighty percent of the last one. That's why your property taxes went down three years ago. We used to have ninety percent coverage—100 percent, after the first thousand.

If I'm closing in on triple digits, near the end of a bad day, I go with some Camus. *One must believe*—scrape—*that Sisyphus*—fling—*is happy*. Plop. But I always save Kierkegaard for 5:00 p.m., whether it's a skunk or a rabbit, a possum or a poodle, a mutt or a fox. *Life can only be understood backwards*—scrape, rump flush to the flange—*but it must be lived*—fling—*forwards*. Plop.

It ain't done it, but I'm finished, at least for another day. I throw in the Removall, check my rearview mirror for anything unlucky enough to be alive, put the engine in gear, and head for the nearest Solid Waste Disposal Field Office. I hose out the bedliner before I drive back to the DOT garage.

They've got cots and a shower—for the nights when we have a Winter Storm Warning. This time of year, nobody cares. I've been sleeping there for the past month, ever since Susan's inner being made friends with the locksmith.

We tried counseling. Or she tried counseling. I went along. I paid. We started coming here right after Thanksgiving. Seven a.m. every Tuesday. That was the only time we both had free. I punch in at nine and she does the lunch-and-dinner shift at Karrie's Kountry Kookhouse. You ever eat there? She's the waitress with the freckles and the frizzy red hair.

They put all of these psych things on the first floor. I guess if somebody jumps out the window, they don't want him crashing through the ceiling of the ER. That's my theory.

I don't think the guy we saw was a real doctor. He must've been a PhD renting office space. No secretary. And no self-respecting shrink would see anyone at seven in the morning unless. . . . Well, the first thing he does is walk around his desk and reach down to hug Susan. He's about six-six and almost as skinny as she is. Then he tries to hug *me*, but I shake his hand before he can wrap my arms up.

"Is everybody here?" he says.

"Excuse me," I say, and I pull Susan back through the doorway. When we're in the corridor, I ask her how she found a marriage counselor who can't count to two.

"Shhhh. He's not a counselor," Susan says. "He's a Relationship Imperfection Coordinator."

Now the guy is right behind us. "Let's establish a lexicon," he says. "I need to know if Every Body is here in a *total* sense. In the sense of the significant presence of their inner being." His left hand sweeps his blond hair out of his eyes. "Doug, we can't find your inner harmony—your inner music—without your inner being to conduct us."

The guy didn't only look like John Tesh—he sounded like him, too. His parents must've played basketball for the Dalai Lama. I asked him if his outer being had a name. When he told me, I said, "I don't want Doctor Jung. I want Doctor Freud." I looked at Susan. "Didn't I tell you? No Jung?"

Hospital Food

"That's Young. With a Y." Now *he* looked at Susan. "Not everybody has found their inner being this morning."

"Everybody," I said, "is singular."

"He has this thing about pronouns," Susan said. "It's been getting worse."

"Between you and I," Doctor Young said, "I think I see your problem."

"No," I said. "I don't think so. Is there a mirror in this room? *I* don't see a mirror in this room. Susan, do *you* see a mirror in this room? Maybe Doctor Young is looking at himself in a mirror that we just can't visually process."

Twenty-two sessions. After Number Fourteen, Susan acknowledged herself for what she was. "Something holy and unquantifiable."

"Try the bathroom scale," I said. "That'll take care of half your problem."

"I embrace myself," Susan said. "I love my own body."

I could've told her that. She'd bought something called a Magic Touch and had been sleeping downstairs since Session Eleven.

"I am embracing myself right now." She was smiling like a Buddhist on Dexatrim.

Then Doctor Young stood up and embraced himself, too. He was the kind of guy who'd hang up mistletoe in a morgue. "Doug, don't you want to join us?"

"No," I said. "I don't."

"This is a very important step for Susan. I wish you'd take a more proactive role in her happiness."

He didn't fool me. I knew he was taking my marriage for a ride on The Porcelain Bus. He was just waiting for the end of the line before pushing the flush button. He spent the next session trying to come up with "a symbol of Susan's inner being that Doug can understand. Something that would convey in his own language the new person Susan has become."

So we stopped having breakfast together at home each Tuesday and drove to the hospital in separate cars.

That's when I started eating here, seven weeks ago. *Twenty-two sessions*—scrape—*at a hundred dollars*—fling—*a pop*. Plop. With eighty percent coverage, I was $440 in the pothole when the outer being of my suitcase appeared on the front lawn. On the same day Susan's inner being changed the locks on the doors.

By then, the girl on the register here could recognize me in her sleep. She's just a kid, maybe eighteen or nineteen. You've seen her. Probably right out of high school.

"Visiting your wife?"

I don't say anything, but I've slid my tray to the dead end of the chrome rails and I can't go anywhere until she rings me up. I'm thinking I must look like something I've pried off Poinsett Highway.

"Cancer?' she asks.

My food's getting cold, so maybe I shrugged my shoulders. Maybe I nodded my head up and down. I don't remember.

"How's her treatment going?"

I don't starve myself like Susan. When I get depressed, I get hungry. With my metabolism, it just doesn't show. My plate's crammed with pancakes, bacon, scrambled eggs, bagels, couple of donuts. OJ and coffee on the side of the tray. Maybe a seven-dollar breakfast. I usually don't eat lunch. I just read in the truck.

"It ain't done it."

"You poor thing." And she rings me up for a dollar. "You come on back, sir. Any time."

So then I start thinking. Seven minus one—that's six dollars a day. Thirty dollars a week. One-twenty a month. If I eat breakfast here until August, I can make it up. I can break even. Not even counting the tips I don't pay.

Hospital food has a bum rap, don't you think? It's not so bad. I mean, it's hard for anyone to ruin *breakfast*. Even Susan couldn't ruin *breakfast*—she just stopped making it when she found her inner being. She's always hated food. That's why she's a good waitress. I could put my thumbs on her belly button and practically reach her backbone with my fingers.

Look at these eggs—not runny, not burned. Ready to shovel right into your mouth. And these pancakes? Don't even need syrup.

Do you cook? Better than this? No kidding. Look, I'm not very good about meeting people. Just tell me one thing. Is your name Susan? Tell me your name isn't Susan. If you're a Susan, then I'm out of here. Poof. Pronto. Scrape. Fling. Plop. No kidding, I'm history.

There's an empty table over by the window. Just say the word. One word.

You a Looney Tune or something? Just tell me your name.

Trash

THEY CALL US THE GAGGERS. Grandfathers Against Garbage. For all I know, you're one of us. Or not. Maybe you're the good ole boy who hauls off my household trash—for free—in an uncovered GMC truck. I've found laminated address labels, on my own Lasix prescriptions, halfway between my home and the county landfill. They didn't get there by themselves.

I've been on the TV. *NewsCenter Now*, *Eyewitness Local*, *Your World at Ten*. They take file footage of our major pickups and save it for a slow day. We go out in groups, with fluorescent orange vests and matching bags. We show up good in color. You'd recognize my face. They like to get me on camera, because I was the first African American optometrist in the state of South Carolina. A little detail that makes the anchors smile and fits into a closing sound bite. "I guess he *sees* about everything out there, Connie." "Read his chart, Nigel. Don't litter." "Dr. Percival Graves, seventy-seven years old, and still keeping his eyes on the prize. Back to you, Tom." On a lot of the pickups, I'm the only black man in sight.

We try to hit the interstate at least three times a year. But for the secondary roads, we'll go it alone, whenever it suits us, in our own neighborhoods. Adopt-A-Spot. It's good exercise, especially in the summer, if you get out early and take it easy. Motion is lotion. Bend your knees. I went to Catholic school in Detroit. When I was a kid, walking home after my last exam in June, I'd always tear my notebooks into confetti and toss them in the gutter. What goes around, comes around. I figure by now I've picked up a few hundred pounds for every ounce I ever dropped. Sister Agatha wouldn't regard me as a complete failure.

No telling what you'll find out here. Condoms, tricycles, forty-pound fertilizer bags, rotary telephones, golf gloves, toilet seats, pajamas. Orphaned shoes—never a pair. Typewriters, clock radios, detached body-side moldings, enough blown truck tires to fill an eighteen wheeler. Whatever it is, we put it in orange bags. Otherwise the DOT workers won't stop on their drive-bys. We use the plastic like Halloween wrapping paper if we run into something really big, like a refrigerator or an old console TV.

Some stuff, it comes along only once. You know it as soon as you see it. A fifty-dollar bill. A dead spider monkey, latched in an aluminum toolbox. *Real* handcuffs. A garment bag stuffed with soiled Pampers, split where it hit the guardrail. A shattered laptop computer with PIECE OF SHIT tattooed on the screen in black nail polish.

Two weeks ago today, I found a water pistol, also black, cunningly molded to look like a forty-five caliber automatic. It had me fooled till I picked it up. I squeezed the trigger. Dry, but it seemed to be in good shape. I put it in my pocket, figured I'd soak it in OxiClean and give it to my grandson the next time he visits. If he visits. . . . His father's not very good about keeping in touch. An investment banker—with a thing for Mickey Mouse! Detroit-Orlando flights don't stop here, though, so they have to make a special trip with a layover if they want to see me on their way to Disney World. They did it every six months when Pearl was alive, but only twice in the past three years, now it's just me and Shadow. I guess I offer them limited options. Picking up garbage and playing with a twelve-year-old dog isn't their idea of The Magic Kingdom.

Two weeks ago today, I was about 500 yards up the road from my house. Shadow pooped out on me, earlier than usual. She does her best to keep up, but twelve is old, even for a little dog, and Shadow weighs fifty pounds. She's on Lasix, too. Congestive heart failure. I was doing what we call a nit pick (cigarette butts and cellophane included). You tell yourself you do a good job everywhere, but everybody's a little more particular around their own home. I was planning to work up to the big oak that marks my property line. Then I'd come back on the Knoblochs' side of the street. It's a neighborly gesture, and I always like to be facing traffic—not that there's much traffic, way out here.

I hear him coming before he rounds the curve, so I drop my orange sack and walk onto the shoulder of the road. A white kid in a primer-red rustbucket Camaro, leaning on his horn and laughing. Doing at least fifty, in a thirty-five-mile zone. After he goes by, I get back to my business, till I hear his half-busted muffler coming back at me from behind.

This time, he's veering left, to the wrong side of the road, to *my* side, and he's got the driver's door wide open. It's like a bullfight, only with the bull dragging the cape and yelling "Nigger!" at the top of his lungs. I scoot over as far as I can against the Ligustrum hedge, and he misses me by three, maybe four feet. Now I hear his brake pads squeak and his transmission thud into reverse. He must be making a K-turn in *my* driveway, getting ready for another pass. I swear aloud. Then a song pops into my head, the Johnny Horton ballad that was always on the office radio the first year I opened my practice—those lines about Andrew Jackson telling his boys not to fire until they could see the eyes of the Redcoats coming toward them.

Redcoats. Rednecks. I drop the bag, I start humming, and I get myself behind the oak tree. It's a big tree, at least two feet in diameter. When he rounds the curve again, I step out and assume the position I see all the time on reruns of *NYPD Blue* and *Homicide* and *Law & Order*—left shoulder pointed forward in the line of fire, barrel just below eye level, left hand steadying the place where my right wrist meets the heel of my palm.

Then, through the windshield, the boy's eyes change.

But he's not looking at me.

I step back behind the tree and turn around. Shadow's in the middle of the road, wheezing and shuffling happily in my direction. I hear the boy's tires scream, but I don't see him hit the power pole on the Knoblochs' side of the street.

Shadow licks my hand like nothing's happened. Gasoline's puddling underneath the Camaro's tailpipe, so I keep my distance from the twisted, steaming metal on the front end. I take out the Senior Center complimentary cell phone that can do one number, 911. And I wait.

§

TRASH

I GUESS YOU COULD SAY I hated him. Or you. As much as you can hate any man you don't really know. He'd been hauling off my household garbage for over thirty years, ever since my optometry practice grew to the point I could afford this place. We'd wanted some land, and back then they wouldn't have let us buy into anything like Belladonna anyway. "Forty acres and a Jeep," I joked to Pearl after we'd moved in. No services, except for electricity and phone. Septic tanks. Well water. Rabbit ears then, DIRECTV now. But you need a special permit to take things to the landfill. So private carriers—that's what they call themselves, carriers—carved up the county and charged what the market would bear.

He wasn't *all* bad. You hear that? Because he never worked on the same day two weeks in a row, he didn't make you bring your cans to the roadside. He'd come up your driveway, in his own sweet time, and take out the sacks himself. Sometimes he'd even put the lids back on the cans. But if I happened to be out working on the lawn, he'd tip his Bullpen College hat on his way by, call me "Governor," and make sure the cans were sideways before he left with the bags.

I tried to get another carrier, but they all told me I was "in Pritchard's district." So I decided to reposition the garbage cans between the house and the road. Not even twenty-five feet up my driveway. I put in some English ivy and built a washed gravel walkway leading to a redwood camouflage enclosure. But in a few weeks, I saw another path beginning to wear through the ground cover, where he was dragging the bags. It was no shorter and no wider than the walkway I'd made just for his godforsaken feet.

I was hopping mad. Pearl begged me to speak with him, politely, to ask him to use the walkway I'd built. She believed in the basic goodness of the human spirit. She'd lived in a world of six-year-olds for forty years. But I couldn't imagine a man doing what *he* was doing out of anything but pure malice. From then on, I had Pearl write out his quarterly checks and mail them to his post office box. Up till the day I retired, I tried not to look off to my left whenever I drove to work. If my eyes wandered in the morning, when Karrie's Kountry Kookhouse brought out my BLT at lunch, I'd still be thinking about bruised leaves, stained with red clay.

§

GAGGERS ARE TIGHT WITH the county police. We see what they do, they see what we do. They try to look out for us. I knew Sandy Blessington, the first officer on the scene. He was one of the first white boys in my "Power to the Pupils" program in the 1960s. It was before integration in the public schools. I'd give free eye exams on Wednesdays to any kid whose teacher thought he couldn't see the blackboard. I'd go straight to any school that would have me, every fall, and I'd make it up on the lenses and frames. Most of the parents, black or white, would be mortified when they got the teacher's note, and they'd want to go high end, to prove they really cared about their kids. But a few didn't care. Sandy's parents wouldn't even sign the note. For years, one ancient lady with a wood-paneled station wagon would ferry those kids to my office, but she'd always wait outside. She'd send them in with cash money. Even the kids didn't know her name. Then one September, she wasn't there anymore. I don't know where she went.

I was holding Shadow safely by the collar while Sandy went about his business. He sprayed some white foam under the chassis, then walked around the perimeter of the old Camaro. When he got to the driver's side, he stuck his hand through the open window and shook his head. I saw more disgust than dismay in the gesture.

Sandy came back to us and called the EMS wagon on his radio. "Take your time. This is recovery. Repeat recovery." Now Sandy was talking to me. "Guess I won, Dr. Graves. We had a bet this kid wouldn't reach twenty."

"What has he done?" I said.

Sandy, a big man who still has his boyhood freckles, was stroking Shadow's head with his open palm. "You tell me, girl." He pushed his polycarbonate lenses back up the bridge of his nose with his other hand. "What hasn't Bo Pritchard done?"

§

IN THE SEVEN YEARS between her retirement and her death, my wife had become one of the most formidable women imaginable—a first-grade teacher with time on her hands. When I sold my practice and retired myself, she was still running half the volunteer activities in the county. In self-defense, I discovered Grandfathers Against Garbage. Now I keep going, like a windup toy.

But first, I had to help her die, piece by piece. I had to pack her wound, after her last surgery. She had an abscess. I'm just an OD—they don't let us operate or prescribe medicine—but I could see that. So I drove her back to the hospital, and I raised hell. She needed to heal up from the inside—otherwise, the poison finds its place, infection works from underneath, and pus bubbles up behind healthy skin. It's not pretty. *Angry* is the word doctors use to describe the site.

The surgeon—probably too lazy to wash his own hands—didn't answer his page. So a third-year resident demonstrated the procedure, then sent us home. Packing strips—thin slivers of sterile gauze. Soap and water around the partially reopened incision. Shove it in with a cotton swab—the wooden end—an inch, a foot, a yard—and bring her pain to the brink of agony, but not beyond. Put on the cotton sponge and tape it lightly—let it leak right through and weep for all who care to see beneath. Or not.

The next day, yank it out like a bloody tapeworm, and start over.

We filled a lot of plastic bags in those days.

All this on the bed where we'd spent forty-five married years. You grit your teeth, stifle a scream, a whimper. All this—to be healed a month before the cancer they couldn't stop stops you. And this is love.

§

MY ROAD IS COVERED with graffiti. (Do you still call it graffiti on a horizontal surface?) Crosses, mainly—white, red, green, blue, yellow. The yellow ones show up best against the asphalt. Not the white. And there are words, too:
BO WE MISS YOU
GOOD OLE BO
ANGEL BO
JESUS LOVES BO
WE REMEMBER

But more than anything else, RIP. These are the letters that seem to draw the most dissenting opinions. RIP—POS. (Does this refer to Bo or to his Camaro, I wonder?) RIP—REAL INTELLIGENT, PRITCHARD. R.I.P. HIM A NEW ONE. And finally, the most brutal revision, the one I wish I'd thought of myself.

RIP—REDNECK IMPROVEMENT PROGRAM.

I wonder how long it will take all this to wash away.

§

AFTER PEARL'S FUNERAL, I started looking at the trampled ivy again, and I put up a split rail fence. I rented a post hole digger and ran the line along the upper edge of the driveway, leaving an opening only for the gravel walkway. The next time Mister Pritchard came into my yard, I saw him stroll up to his self-made path and take the two rails from between their posts. After he'd dragged six bags down—I'd cleaned out Pearl's closets—he put the rails back, turned toward the living-room window, and saluted where I was standing between the curtains.

I made it down the driveway before he'd gotten back into his truck. "Mister Pritchard," I said.

"Governor," he said.

"I've decided I can no longer afford your services."

"That what you decided?"

"Yes. You can keep the money for this quarter."

"Shoot, Governor." He took off his cap and bowed. *Bowed*. "I can service you free."

"I don't want you on my property, Mister Pritchard."

He got back into his truck and threw what was left of his coffee onto the concrete. "Working man don't get no respeck in this world." He made the word sound like a bug on a windshield. My windshield. "No respeck."

§

TO SEE COLORS, to see them truly, you need light. Lots of light. But on moonless evenings, there's another world outside my living room window. Some nights, I want to be part of it, that parade of grays, subtle as the texture of a good suit. And my suit is this: Why do we call it "a matter of black and white" when we're dreaming of absolute clarity? Black and white is a complicator, a distortion, a world of empty shapes that whisper in the shadows, becoming not what we see, but what we've convinced ourselves is there: lawn, driveway, redwood retainers, garbage cans, split rail fence.

I remember when television was black and white. Pearl did, too. We grew up with radio, then we switched over to TV in the 1950s. Watched a lot of it. We weren't church people. Near the end, to keep herself from screaming, she'd recite old commercials, over and over. *Crest is an effective decay-preventive dentifrice that can be of significant value when used in a conscientiously applied program of oral hygiene and regular professional care. Aero Wax—So Tough, Bullets Bounce Off! Mother, please, I'd rather do it MYSELF! Coke—The Pause That Refreshes.* And finally, before the narcotics reduced her to a meaningless stupor: *Timex—Takes a Lickin' and Keeps on Tickin'.* She was a remarkable woman. We moved down here, where our great-grandparents had been slaves, to make a difference in people's lives. She did.

§

SOMETIMES I SIT in my basement garage, in my RX 300, just like the Lexus ad told me I would, and listen to a world class stereo. The FM scanner button gives me all that America has to offer, in five second riffs: R&B, NPR, today's country, Atlanta Braves baseball, breaking news, rap, holy roller, soft rock, hard rock, classic rock, classic country, the golden age of radio, all talk all the time. Whenever I hear a commercial, I think of Pearl, and I wonder if she heard that particular vain, silly jingle while she was on this earth.

"Upside down," Sandy Blessington said, grimly laughing. "His watch was on upside down."

"Upside down," I said.

"Upside down," I say now, to the skimming green numbers on my radio, in my empty car.

And this is life.

§

Years ago, long before we left Detroit, the house I live in belonged to a white man who owned half the county. He drank away all but these forty acres, then promised his wife he'd get on the wagon. But he couldn't. So he'd drive up the mountain to buy hip flasks of moonshine he could drink in secret, at one sitting. He'd heave the empties as far back as he could, into his own woods. He could've tossed them anywhere, but he didn't. For thirty-five springs, while I've been out gathering winter-dead branches for the brush pile, I've found them, pushing up from the soil like amber daffodils. Immortality takes many forms. When Shadow dies, I've decided to bury her under the best unbroken bottle I see.

§

After the EMS wagon left, I told Sandy Blessington what had really happened. Showed him the pistol I'd pointed. And I told him I was going to speak to Bo Pritchard's father.

"You're not making good sense, Dr. Graves."

"I'm not?"

"You said it yourself. Bo didn't see you. He swerved to avoid Shadow here."

I told him he swerved *after* he saw me. I told him if I hadn't pointed that gun, Bo Pritchard might still be alive.

"Look, if it was a real gun, and you'd a shot him, it'd still be self-defense. He came at you. Three times. A motor vehicle is a deadly weapon. No sense in begging Mister to sue you. He'd lose anyway. I guarantee it."

"No respeck," I said.

Sandy Blessington nodded. "Little cracker had it coming."

§

Then Shadow started following me around the house, even more closely than usual. When I do the vacuuming, every other day, she usually hides in the basement till I'm finished. So you can imagine my surprise when she started mounting the nearest sofa or bed—lifting her front legs, then painfully hauling the rest of her body after her—and circling around, pointing her nose in my direction, letting her big ears flop on either side of her muzzle. Maybe, I thought, she can't hear the vacuum cleaner anymore.

But she can hear thunder.

Back when the *Homicide* series was still on NBC, I always identified with Detective Frank Pembleton. A man, with skin darker than my own, who loves his wife and family. Who believes in an evil that has no color, an evil that must be resisted. He makes his living by coming to logical conclusions, by seeing clearly, in a small room just the size of my very first office. He never needed his gun.

Last Tuesday, I was watching the made-for-TV-movie sequel, when I finally realized something. I'm more like Frank's boss—Captain Giardello. He's about to become mayor, not governor. Close enough. Somebody else, just my color, who had a wife and family. But his wife's dead. And his son, his Mike, won't speak to him.

In the movie, G—that's what they call him, G—is destroyed by a gun. For seeing too clearly. I watched his spirit, or whatever was left of it, playing cards in what had become his eternal home—the Baltimore police station. Only the dead will speak to him. The living pass, ghosts laminated on the present, unable to see. Mike, just like the rest.

A flash of lightning from my own window caught the corner of my eye.

But G kept playing cards.

When the BOOM sounded, shaking the house to its foundation, the TV went dead. Shadow had run off. I thought I should check out the connection to the satellite dish, to make sure the surge protector had done what it's supposed to do. When I walked over the rug where she'd been lying down, I felt Shadow's warm urine on my bare feet.

From there I could see her in the kitchen, sprawled on the white ceramic tile. Looking like nothing had happened. And I knew what I had to do. I dragged her by the collar back into the living room, and I stuck her nose into her own mess. Then she pissed again, right where she was standing, and her whole body sagged down.

I couldn't stop myself. I saw the empty water pistol on the credenza, and I smacked her on the rump, over and over. She finally bit my wrist, best as she could, then hobbled down the basement steps.

"You're dead," I whispered, putting the pistol back where I'd found it. "Dead."

Pearl would have been ashamed of me.

§

TOMORROW—AND FOR YOU, it is at least tomorrow—I will take Shadow to the vet. I will try to explain her problem. I will pay for his professional judgment. And then I will take her home—perhaps in a suitable plastic bag, to bury her deep in my own woods, under the most beautiful bottle I can find. But probably just on her old leash, to banish her to the basement, where her shaky bladder can't harm a sealed concrete floor, a water heater, a washer/dryer combination, or an old Underwood typewriter I'd forgotten I ever owned.

I will tape these pages to a garbage bag that will be thrown in the back of a battered GMC truck, and buffeted out in the breeze on the way to the landfill.

Or not.

I have a theory. Let's call it a philosophy. Any living creature deserves at least two chances. You're either within ten point four miles of my driveway, or one hundred feet from my front porch. In either case, I am Dr. Percival Graves. The first African American optometrist in the state of South Carolina. When I retired, there still weren't even 250 of us in the entire country.

I don't keep count anymore.

I'm in the telephone book. I'm also in the basement, with Shadow at my feet. Losing at solitaire. Or not. If you're in my driveway, or if you're walking against traffic, you should be pointed in the right direction. The cellar door is unlocked. You might hear the radio in the Lexus, shuffling through every station with a strong enough signal, trying to find something, behind the paneling that separates me from the garage.

Right now, I can hear Pearl's sweet voice: *Who knows what goodness lurks in the hearts of men?*

Who knows.

Standard Kung Fu Mayhem

Scene One

ON OPPOSITE SIDES OF A small, square table, Mr. Magee and his Executive Intern sat in the restaurant of the Greenville-Spartanburg Airport. Ten minutes ahead of schedule, they were waiting for a screenwriting consultant unlucky enough to live in South Carolina. Juliette could feel her shoulder blades sticking to her new silk blouse—the local air conditioning had gone on summer vacation. But for the grace of God, she could've ended up licking envelopes for a non-profit agency in a no-place like this. To keep her mind off the heat, she fast-forwarded through her considerable blessings, while her boss was indulging himself in a post-production review of their recently completed LAX-to-Atlanta-to-Greenville flight.

"I didn't insist on the private jet. Hey, I'm a regular guy. Ask anybody in the business. Did I complain in LA? Did I complain?"

"You didn't complain," Juliette said. Mr. Magee seemed to like hearing his questions repeated as definitive statements.

"I can handle First Class, Juliette. I handle First Class all the time. Then Atlanta dumps us into that puddle jumper, right next to Jihad Kaboom."

"The guy in the white serape?" Although she'd completed her second year of Communication Studies at a small college in Sacramento, Juliette had grown up in Lubbock, Texas, in an emerging multicultural environment. When she'd mentioned this fact to Mr. Magee, during her interview at Digital Donnybrook Productions, he hadn't believed her. He'd insisted on seeing her driver's license for verification. Then he'd muttered that she didn't *look* old enough to be an organ donor. After her solemn assurance that her organs were indeed under her personal control, he'd hired her for twenty dollars an hour, for the whole summer.

"Whatever," Magee said. He wiped his wide, sun-freckled brow with his cloth napkin. "I thought Juan Valdez was gonna break into the cockpit and fly us into that goddamn peach. It wouldn't've taken a major course change."

While they'd been circling to land at GSP, the pilot—a woman—had banked the small plane sharply, to give the starboard passengers a better view of the Gaffney water tower. Its crowning Freestone, Juliette remembered, had a tiny dimple and a small green leaf.

"Did you see the soles of his shoes?"

"The soles of his shoes," Juliette said.

"You could've wedged a couple sticks of dynamite in there."

She took two menus from the triple-chinned waitress and passed one of them to Mr. Magee. Intermediary Handling. It was part of her job description. Her boss glanced at the laminated plastic and rolled his eyes. "This everything?"

"You caught us between dinner and supper, sir."

"Lost your lunch, Harriet?" He turned from her name tag to look at the unbroken expanse of runway beyond the tinted glass. "Why they call this place Windows?"

"Our grilled chicken salad is on special."

Juliette said, "I'll take that, with the raspberry vinaigrette."

"Something to drink, honey?" Harriet said.

"Unsweet tea."

"What else you got? To drink," Magee said.

"Sweet tea."

"Make it a double."

The coffee-colored waitress beamed under her big hair, tore off their order slip, and leaned it against the combination salt-and-pepper shaker before she left for the kitchen. "Windows for Greenville," Magee laughed. "Sounds like Microsoft for Mental Defectives. Every cunt in this town wears cubic zirconia and smiles like a hyena with a carcass. They won't even tell me to go fuck myself. Drives me nuts."

Juliette could understand his frustration. In less than a full week, she'd already discovered that Mr. Magee had a formidable talent: He could make anybody swear at him, at any time. "How often do you come here?"

"That depends," Magee grinned. "Looking for a performance bonus?"

Before Juliet could answer definitively, the waitress returned with their drinks. "I asked for a double, honey," Magee said. "Bring me another glass." He peeled the paper off the tip of his straw, took a short swig, and grimaced.

"Lemme warn you. This guy we're hooking up with, he's a real nutcase. Never takes credit for *anything*. But he's been in the business forever. Fucking genius. He only works here, and he only works face to face. Like he's afraid you're gonna die—before you can pay him?"

"Before you can pay him," Juliette agreed.

"I'm strictly high concept," Magee said. "Maybe half of my movies, Charley's goosed the endings. Classic lines. And not just for me, either. *Do you feel lucky, punk? I'll be back. Yippy Ki Yay, motherfucker.* They're all his."

Her boss liked to exaggerate, so Juliette still didn't know what to think when the waitress returned with her salad and the extra iced tea.

"We're waiting for a third wheel," Magee said. "Nice rock you got there, honey."

"Biggest they had," the waitress said. "Fifty percent off." She put the brimming glass in front of the open chair without spilling a drop. Then she extended her left hand, palm down, milk chocolate fingers spread. "Demarcus gifted me last Christmas."

"Now *that's* a husband. Somebody who gets his rocks half off at a Mall Mart." After their waitress had left, with her smile still intact, Magee said, "See what I mean?"

"I see what you mean."

Juliette had nearly finished her salad when an old man limped past the register station, into her line of sight. He recognized her boss from behind, and spoke his name. Magee was talking to an executive producer on his cell phone, so he stuck the index finger of his free hand straight up, then angled it toward the unoccupied glass of iced tea. The man lowered his laptop computer to the sloppily seamed carpet tiles before he sat down.

Juliette couldn't resist. "Did you *really* write *Yippy Ki Yay mother—*"

The old man stopped her with his eyes, which then scanned the vast, empty room. "I had help with that one," he whispered.

"That scene is so awesome." Juliette found herself whispering, too. "When Bruce Willis is laying on the runway, and he torches that jet fuel leading to the terrorists' plane—I mean, it's one of the defining moments in modern American cinema."

"Thank you."

"I studied it in college. Spring term. *Introduction to Action Adventure*. Okay, I signed up because it's a requirement for my major, but then I got hooked, you know? That's how I landed this internship with Mr. Magee. Engaged Learning," she explained.

Magee pocketed his cell phone. "Sorry, Charley. Frigging producers. You get my email?"

"Yes, Mr. Magee."

"Guy's a frigging genius, and he calls me Mr. Magee. *Mister* Magee." Magee grinned at Juliette. "Didn't I tell you Charley Harris was a frigging genius?"

She simply nodded her head. When her boss had studiously avoided the *f*-word, Juliette had been too stunned to speak.

Magee clapped his hands. "So you know the scenario. Mid-budget chop-socky, Charley. We're looking for something that pushes PG-13 but doesn't drop an R. So the junior high kids can put one over on their parents. Think you can handle it?"

"I've already handled it." He passed a typescript to Juliette. After she'd passed it over to Magee, he pulled out another hard copy for her, and she began to read.

Anglo Hero enters abandoned warehouse at midnight. Dim security lighting. Suspense. Cut to Korean mobster and his twin sister, crouching behind a crate marked POKET CALULATORS. They step out from either side of the crate.

"AIEEE!" Hero tilts torso left, to evade flying sister. "AIEEE!" Hero tilts torso right, as mobster brother flies by. Hero grins at camera. Three minutes of standard kung fu mayhem. Hero power-kicks

sister into crate, scattering substandard third-world electronic equipment over blast radius of thirty feet.

Hero approaches her, at a deliberate pace. Mobster brother tries frantically to pursue, but slips and falls on pocket calculator. Hero handcuffs left wrist of dazed sister to nearby forklift. Hero turns to face brother. Hero's face suddenly changes from supreme confidence to slight confusion. Hero looks slowly downward, until he sees sister's foot lodged between his legs.

Hero whispers "AIEEE?" Hero grabs sister's foot and twists it until, with a decisive snap, it rotates 180 degrees from its customary position.

Sister screams "AIEEE!"

Hero drops sister's foot and pursues mobster brother once more. Three minutes of climactic kung fu mayhem. Hero punishes every part of mobster's body, except groin. Mobster finally collapses, backwards, unconscious, before Hero's triumphant scowl.

"You no lead him his lights!" sister screams. "We cop suey!"

Hero smiles, then puts an exploratory Nike in supine mobster's crotch.

One pocket calculator crash-lands, to Hero's left. Another, to Hero's right.

"No statisticals!" Jump cut to sister's screaming face, as she picks up more calculators to heave at Hero. "No statisticals!"

"And a one," Hero declaims, transferring weight to front foot.

"No statisticals!"

Hero readjusts Nike. "And a two."

CHAMPAGNE CORK POPS. ROLL TO CREDITS. LAWRENCE WELK MUSIC THROUGHOUT, PUNCTUATED BY CRIES OF "HELLO, HAPPY PEOPLE" AND "AIEEE!"

She looked up from her hard copy. Mr. Magee must have been waiting for her to finish before pronouncing his judgment. "Unbelievable! Every Mongoloid in America will be acting this out in his algebra class!" He stood up in the empty restaurant and screamed in falsetto, "*No statisticals!*" Now he returned to his customary pitch. "You can't *buy* publicity like that. Not to mention the potential synergy with Texas Instruments." Magee gazed at Juliette. "There's a problem?"

Visual Confirmation. That was in her job description, too. "There's a problem," Juliette stared back, without blinking. "The dog."

"Good girl," Magee said.

Charley rubbed his sparse eyebrows. "You didn't tell me about a dog."

"Well, I figured we'd work it out here," Magee said. "You've given us some great stuff. For the sequel. But for now . . . ."

Charley simply drank his sweet tea, but Juliette could've sworn he was thinking. Finally, when he got to the point where he was sucking up mostly ice melt through his translucent straw, he said, "Why do you need a dog?"

"Canine buddy xenophobic chop-socky." Magee adjusted his gaze. "Virgin territory?"

"Never been done," she confirmed.

Magee continued. "While this cop's beating up on the Korean mob, his cocker spaniel follows him around. Lots of *mise en scène* shit with the dog. You know. Barks. Whimpers. Crotch licking. Paws over the eyes. Then, for the finale, the dog does the *coup de grâce*. You figure out how."

Charley swirled the straw in his sweaty glass. "Could you make it a cat?"

Magee shrugged, and told Juliette he'd defer to her judgment. She was a lot closer to thirteen than he was.

"Could I borrow your cell?" Juliette didn't want to waste her own minutes on Digital Donnybrook business. "I'll call my kid brother."

"How about *two* cats?" Charley suggested. "Eastwood and Willis?"

Juliette stopped in mid-punch, nearly dropping the tiny phone into her salad plate.

"I told you!" Magee shouted, slamming his palm on the table. "Guy's a frigging genius!"

But Charley was already at work on his laptop. When he'd finished, Juliette stood over Magee's shoulder, so they could both view the screen.

This time, it's a supermarket warehouse with a crate full of PRE-MIUM CAT FOOD. The villains wear baggy ghetto pants as they fly past. Eastwood and Willis meow in unison, giving Anglo Hero a paws-up while he kicks the sister into the crate. Kibbles scatter everywhere. Hero handcuffs the sister's ankles together, behind her head, and says, "Don't move." After her brother finally collapses, Eastwood and Willis sit on his chest.

"You no lead him his lights!" sister screams. "We cop suey!" Sister drags herself to an open crate of canned cat food. She starts throwing 3-ounce containers at Hero. Eastwood and Willis wander away.

Hero picks up container and says, "Tasty Tenders." Hero pulls aluminum tab, lifts the waistband of mobster's baggy pants, and dumps food inside. "Oh Eastwood! Oh Willis!" Hero holds open both legs of mobster's ghetto pants at the ankles. Following their nostrils, the cats approach slowly, from opposite directions.

More cans strike around Hero.

"No catstray! No catstray!"

Eastwood and Willis have become large, invisible lumps, moving up mobster's legs. Hero makes certain that mobster's black belt is secure.

"No catstray!"

Jump cut to mobster's face. His eyes suddenly open.

"Eastwood, meet Willis," Hero declaims.

Opening eight notes from "The Good, the Bad, and the Ugly" theme, while the two bulges meet beneath the baggy pants.

"AIEEE!"

ROLL TO CREDITS. EASTWOOD AND WILLIS ACAPPELLA.

Magee was applauding, with his wallet already in his hands. The muffled thumps sounded like someone hitting a sorority pledge with a paddle. "Both endings, Charley! How much?"

"The usual. Times two."

"Fair enough. And as far as I'm concerned, it's all under the radar. Geeks at the IRS, they like their Adult Entertainment. They owe me. Big time."

But Charley wouldn't take cash. And why did he insist on *two* checks? Both payable to him? Frigging genius, Juliette decided, was something no nineteen-year-old organ donor needed to understand. That was the beauty of Engaged Learning.

§

Scene Two

HE MANAGED TO GET INSIDE the Bank of Belladonna branch office on Woodruff Road three minutes before it closed. He countersigned both checks FOR DEPOSIT ONLY and put them into separate accounts that bore the same name—Charles Harris—but different Social Security numbers. He asked the teller for deposit slips with the current balance for each account. When he saw they matched, right down to the penny, he thanked the young woman for her patience. It was already 5:05. "Just doing my job," she declared. But she followed him to the tempered glass door and locked it behind him as he left the building. The man didn't take it personally. It wasn't his usual branch. Here, he was just another stranger.

Outside, the soiled cotton-candy clouds had lowered into a slow, steamy drizzle. He shivered, despite the heat, as he walked past the ATM machines to his Volvo 850. In the mist, it looked like an abandoned refrigerator turned sideways. It was the safest car on the road when he'd bought it ten years ago. But now? He'd have to Google it.

He twisted his light stick, then put the intermittent wipers on their lowest setting. When he got back on I-385, he continued driving south. He passed a few cars until he came up behind a minivan with glowing taillights. The mist was getting denser, more opaque. He trailed behind, close enough to see the red halos, far enough away to stop, if he had to, in plenty of time.

As he looked ahead, he tried to keep his mind empty. But he couldn't help wondering what would become of Mr. Magee's latest canary in the mineshaft of modern American demographics. A blond, beautiful child, determined to grow up by yesterday afternoon. He thought of Shakespeare's Juliet, and Friar Lawrence with a leer and a $10,000 hairpiece. Then he imagined Mr. Magee at something called the *Lay-Ze-Boy Dude Ranch And Bordello* in Climax, Nevada, talking ponies and perversions with his own ex-wife, telling her that Charley Harris didn't know what bliss he was missing. Charley laughed aloud. Only God knew what Margitte was doing now. And with whom. He hadn't seen her since—he tried to remember the year. He couldn't.

His mind drifted into the mist beyond his windshield. Now he saw himself younger, much younger, inside a circle of five-gallon industrial buckets, under the suffering live oak in their back yard in Belladonna. The Drought That Wouldn't End. He'd punched two small holes in the bottom of each bucket, then filled them, brimming, with water from the black rubber hose every morning. The most efficient way to safeguard a big tree. He'd read about it in a gardening book, before computers . . . .

He was pulling into the trailer park, with no recollection of the last miles he'd driven. It had stopped raining, and the only water still standing slunk in the culverts flanking the gravel road. After he pulled underneath his fiberglass carport, he cut off the engine and felt the parking brake click into place beneath his hand. He closed and reopened his eyes. Something metallic was ticking, erratically, like a broken egg timer. For the rest of the day, he told himself, he would remember everything. He would see, hear, smell, or taste every contingency. Nothing would escape his attention. Nothing.

Tomasa met him at the door. She was a stout, thirtyish woman with stained teeth that almost exactly matched the color of her skin. "Mr. Charley!" She freed the laptop from his hand and looked back over her shoulder. "Your father is home!" The woman walked with him into a long, narrow room filled with Scotchgarded sofas and chairs. Cartoons were blaring from behind a closed door. "I can stay until six-forty-five," she said. "He never take his bath if you no here."

"Sorry," he said. "Complications."

"Tell me about it," Tomasa smiled. She tapped the highest button of her blouse three times. "*Tres hijos*. Mr. Charley, I know the complications. But my husband is early from the Belladonna today. He no can roof in the rain. He can handle thirty minutes." She walked to the bedroom door, opened it, and shouted over the television. "Charley, your father is home! I put your pajamas next to the sink."

The cartoons poofed into silence. Tomasa came back out of his son's room, reaching up to guide Charley by one shoulder. His son's other arm lagged behind at its customary, bizarre angle, a hieroglyphic that defied translation. "Hi, Daddy!" Charley shouted. "You make my day!"

"Hi, Junior." He walked up to Charley and ruffled what was left of his son's hair.

Tomasa led his son down the short hallway. Charley shuffled from the carpet to the ceramic tile, his Spiderman slippers barely clearing the threshold strip. While the spigots creaked open, a scruffy head popped out again through the doorway. "I'll be back!"

Because three people couldn't fit inside the trailer's bathroom, he sat down in his recliner with the local newspaper, and he pretended to read. After a long drive, his bad foot always felt better when he fully extended his legs. The sound of splashing water came through the sheetrock behind his head. Tomasa was laughing. "Clean yourself, Charley. Or I have to clean for you."

"No statisticals! No statisticals!"

"Then you wash," Tomasa said. "You take the rag."

Ten minutes later, Charley emerged—his skin still warm-water rosy where his neck peeked out from his collar, where his hairy wrists stuck out from the ends of his flannel sleeves. "I don't like these," Charley said. "I want Spidermans!"

"They don't make those pajamas in your size," he said. "I'm sorry."

"Sorry. Sorry Charley. Spiderman is big, too."

"Not as big as you, son."

Tomasa checked to see that all Charley's buttons were fastened. After she sat him down at the breakfast bar with his spill-proof cup, she whispered, "I make him pajamas, Mr. Charley. For his birthday."

"They have Spiderman fabric now?" He looked up from the Lifestyles section, which he had just begun to read. Tomasa's brown eyes were brimming with light.

"In Mall Mart I see the bedsheets. Cotton. One hundred percent. I can use them. Mr. Charley, you pay me so much. It is a little I can do."

He'd moved to this trailer park, twelve years ago, because it was the only place he'd discovered where no one—no one—ever tormented his child. Tomasa lived a half-dozen families away, with her own family. With Jorge and their *tres hijos*—boys who looked like Guatemalan translations of Russian dolls when they stood side by side. She'd been helping him ever since he'd broken his foot trying to get his own son out of the bathtub. "I'll buy the bedsheets," he promised. "Go home. It's seven o'clock."

"The food is in the blue dish. Auto Reheat. Five minutes."

"Thank you, Tomasa. *Gracias.* Now go home."

She'd made a rice casserole with chicken, in a white sauce that didn't stain Charley's pajamas. After they'd finished, he filled two plastic bowls with cat food and watched his son put them out on the front porch.

"Oh catstrays!" His son was shouting as if he wanted every small animal in the world to hear him. "Oh catstrays!"

Eastwood, an old ginger-colored tabby, came slinking up the stairs first. When Charley unfolded his arm and dangled it behind the cat's ears, he said, "Be careful, son." Eastwood sprawled on the poured concrete, his big front paws hanging over the lip of his dish. Willis, late as usual, preferred to chew standing up.

"Time for dessert, Charley." They left the cats outside, licking their bowls. When they got to the kitchen, he opened the refrigerator and took out a tall can of whipped cream. He shook it to make sure it was fully loaded. Then, like a gunfighter, he drew it up from his belt and pointed the nozzle at his son's face. "You've had this coming for a long time, mister."

"If you're going to shoot, SHOOT!" Charley said. He opened his mouth so wide that his father could see the big fillings in his bottom molars. "Don't talk!"

He pressed the plastic tip until his son's tongue disappeared under a white swoosh. Charley swallowed, licked his lips clean, and said, "Do you feel lucky?"

"Time for bed, Junior. Man's got to know his limitations."

After his son was under the covers, he sat on the edge of the mattress. He pulled out his wallet and cross-checked the deposit slips, to make sure he had the right one. Then he closed his son's fingers around the slick, shadowy paper. "Good job, buddy."

"Good job, Daddy!" Beneath the bedsheets, Charley's legs were twitching at the random, familiar angles. *Exaggerated deep tendon reflexes*, the Spasticity Clinic had said. They had a name for everything, and a cure for nothing.

"Say your prayers, Charley."

"Now I lay me down to sleep, I pray the Lord my soul to keep, and if I die before I wake, I pray the Lord my soul to take. God bless Eastwood, and Willis, and Arnold, and Norris, and Daddy, and Mommy." He reached over to his nightstand and picked up a washed-out Kodachrome of a young woman sitting on a pony, holding a laughing toddler in her lap.

Twelve months after she'd started giving riding lessons at the local equestrian park.

Six months after she'd come home to find their son, outside, under the oak tree, in their back yard with the new security fencing, while his father was lost in a screenplay whose title even God had forgotten, and whose options had not been renewed.

Five months after the doctors had told them that more toddlers drown in big buckets than in salt water.

Three months after he'd come off the ventilator, out of the coma, and miraculously spoken their names.

Two months after they'd taken him home—to a front yard full of Belladonna neighbors and banners and balloons!

Eight months before he'd passed all the "developmental milestones" that he ever would.

Twelve months before a counselor had told them that seventy-six percent of all marriages survive a "near drowning incident" and she'd said, "That leaves twenty-four percent."

Eighteen months before Margitte had told him that she couldn't live with the tricks he kept playing on the world—a broken bucket that had turned their son into something less than the beasts she guided to and from the stable each day.

Twenty-one months before he'd shouted that *she'd* thought the buckets were a good idea, too. She'd begged him to move to

Belladonna. She'd fallen in love with that live oak tree for its "curb appeal." Where was her wisdom *then*?

Charley was smudging the glass with his lips. "Yippy Ki Yay, Mommy! Yippy Ki Yay!"

He took the frame by the edges and wiped the glass clean with a tissue. "That's right, Charley." He stared at the radiant face of the wife, of the mother, who'd finally ridden out of their lives. A posed picture. The backdrop, of course, was painted—a snowy mountain in the distance, shimmering like an exotic, unreachable dessert. "Yippy Ki Yay." But he couldn't speak the obscenity, the one word that had become his enduring, anonymous contribution to American culture.

For five minutes, his son pretended to be asleep. To be more than asleep. It was his favorite game, the one he played every night. Loud, gurgling, gasping snores, then silence. It always ended the same way. "I'm dead," Charley announced, his eyes scrunched tight while his lips moved. "Are you dead yet?"

His father kissed him on his unshaven cheek. He turned off the light on the nightstand and pressed his own lips together in the new dark. Then he stood up from the bedside and wondered if Mr. Magee—if anybody—would ever bring him a script worthy of the six endless words that his beautiful child had become.

Inflatable Kids

THE MORNING FOG WAS STILL HEAVY, and the red clay road was getting worse. I pretended I was riding a horse, posting, pressing my rump on the invisible saddle bouncing above my banana seat. But the ruts were shooting up the handlebars into my shoulders. I'd have to take four ibuprofen—my wife Elise calls it Vitamin I—when I got home.

When we'd lived on the other end of the county, I didn't even know there were any dirt roads left between here and the North Carolina line. But after we'd sold the pet store and moved to where the malls ended and the mountains began, I found out that the city of Greenville was still just a small island of quiche in a sea of grits and red-eye gravy. They didn't call these foothills The Dark Corner for nothing.

I hadn't seen a soul since I'd turned off Highway 25—just the body of a pit bull that filled my nostrils a minute before I got to it and another minute after I'd passed. Then a single-wide trailer with the roof caving into its rust, its front door hanging from a lonely hinge. I could've torn it loose on the way by.

The fog was brightening, getting ready to burn off. The sun wasn't a disk yet, but you could tell where it was going to come through. I could start to make out the kudzu and honeysuckle smothering the scrub pines on my left side.

Then the road ended in an eight-foot chain-link fence.

Even though I was coasting, I had to use all of my brakes to stop short. I got off my bike and leaned it on the ground. The fence looked new, topped by two strands of barbed wire that hadn't had time to rust. Near the padlocked gate to the gravel driveway, an oversized mailbox stood inside a metal cage welded from short segments of iron pipe. The mailbox door had a horizontal slit for letters, just below another combination Master Lock.

I took off my helmet and rested my forehead against the fence. I have to admit I was curious about the kind of landscaping anyone would do out here. A fescue lawn? Naturalized azaleas and rhododendrons beneath some white dogwoods? Or bare dirt swept smooth, under a wide-spreading oak?

What I saw was sand. The kind of sand you find at a children's playground—fine, clean, meant to keep knees and elbows from getting scraped and little sneakers from getting muddy. In the distance—maybe fifty feet away—I could make out a boy in shorts and a T-shirt on a teeter-totter. A bit further back, I saw what could have been his older brother, in blue overalls, balanced on top of a metal slide.

Both of them had their hands raised, so I waved back. "That looks like fun!" I shouted. Now I could dimly make out the house, which was the standard red brick, three-bedroom you'll see in any starter subdivision in South Carolina. We'd lived in one for years. Out here, though, it looked like a mansion.

I was about to ask the boy on the teeter-totter if he'd like my ballast on the other end of the board. Then I noticed a tire valve coming out of the side of his brother's neck.

Frankenstein meets Tom Sawyer.

I got back on my bike, and I didn't stop to put on my helmet until I could smell that dead dog again.

§

NINE MONTHS AGO, my wife and I moved into the SwanSong Retirement Learning Community. Elise got hooked by the developer's sign—those two birds molded into the big *S*'s—and by the free classes offered by the local college that was fronting the construction costs. You see it happening all over the country now. They must figure all the old geezers will love their little one-story ivory towers enough to rewrite their wills before The Final Exam.

They've got patio homes, condos, assisted living, basic hospice, even a short-term infirmary on-site. You move into whatever you can handle, and then they switch you around as "your life situation matures." We got the pre-construction price after we'd sat through the sales pitch at the college development office—even though the VP was visibly disappointed when we told him we were only 58. He perked up, though, when Elise mentioned we were *sans enfants*.

"Does your college offer advanced courses in *littérature française*?" Elise had asked.

The VP smiled broadly. "*Bien sur*, Madame Michel."

"Do you allow dogs and cats? Like Belladonna Assisted Living?"

"*Mais non. Pour des raisons de sant*é."

Elise had looked at me triumphantly. "The patio home."

"We'll take it," I said.

We'd married right out of high school in Painted Post, New York, and worked at my family's horse farm—until we got a long-distance call from a lawyer who sounded like Andy Griffith. Elise's grandfather had died and left us a pet store. *My Beloved Dimples*, that's what his will said, though he hadn't seen her in twenty years. Nobody local wanted to buy it, or even run it, so we'd moved to Greenville and scraped by until urban renewal started. Elise got the idea of turning it into *Le Faux Roar*. A cat specialty shop. We'd trademarked our logo—a marmalade American Shorthair with his mouth wide open, peeking out from a lion's mane. Last August, a venture capitalist from Connecticut bought us out on the spot. He'll be starting a nationwide franchise as soon as he's completed the marketing surveys.

I'd always handled the accounting, and Elise had dealt with the animals. "I've spent most of my life shoveling cat poop," Elise had reminded me, after we'd signed and mailed the last papers to Connecticut. "Now I want to read Proust."

So the new Elise has a *Remembrance of Things Pasta* cookbook, we eat madeleines instead of Krispy Kreme donuts, and she spends most of the day doing her homework assignments. I ride my bike every morning and play golf three times a week, when I join her on the shuttle van to campus.

I like the new Elise, so I haven't been able to tell her I think we made a mistake. About half the units are occupied now, and we're the only ones here under eighty. "More younger people will move in," Elise assures me. "And we'll get older."

In the meantime, everyone waves at us. Mr. Gordon, the white-suited bachelor with the polished brass walker. Frau Bauman, the widow who's trying to teach him to give her simple commands in German. Mr. and Mrs. Pedersen, who walk shoulder to shoulder, their hands clasped together, past our house every evening, off to feed the swans—*if* they can agree on the right direction. We wave back. We say *Gesundheit* whenever it seems appropriate. We point out the way to the artificial pond. Nobody remembers our names.

There's an ad for the upgraded hospice service in the fitness center. *Extremely Generous Medication Protocols! We're Changing America, One Person at a Time!* A couple of weeks ago, I crossed out *Person* and wrote in *Corpse*. If anyone's noticed, they haven't told me yet.

§

ELISE GOT DOWN FROM her own ten-speed at the turnoff. She was staring at a shredded tire lying on the side of the road like a dead crow.

"I'm not driving a bike in there. *Pas du tout.*"

"Why don't we walk them in?" I said.

At times like this, I wish we hadn't sold our twin Audis. Swan-Song believes in sustainability—no garages, electric shuttle buses—and Elise had insisted upon simplifying our golden years. "Now I know how Paris felt in the summer of 1944," Elise had said, waving her newly-cut Carmax cashier's check at me. And, to be honest, I have to say the idea appealed to a part of me too. "We got no car," I'd tentatively warbled. "Got no mule," she'd sung. "Got no *mis-er-y*," we'd harmonized together, clinking our wine glasses in front of the remote-controlled gas fireplace, before we'd shucked each other's clothes like a couple of horny teenagers.

But marching a Schwinn down a red-clay road in the middle of June wasn't Elise's notion of The Simple Life. I'd warned her about the pit bull, so she'd brought her nose clips and looked the other way. Possums must have been busy from the night before, though. Not much more than the bones and the dark muzzle remained.

We're both in good shape, but it took us nearly half an hour to get to the dead end. When she saw the mailbox cage, she said, "I wonder if it's booby-trapped."

"It can't be," I said, twirling the knob on the cylinder lock. "The mailman has to get in there every day."

The children had moved. Now one of them was in a swing set, and the other was poking his head out of the end of a fifteen-foot plastic tube painted to look like a big worm. "See the air valves?" I said. "Right below the ears."

"Anybody home?" Elise yelled. She rattled the metal gate at the end of the driveway before looking back at me. "That's one hell of a motorcycle he's got in the carport."

I walked up behind her and peered over the top of her head. A flame-painted Suzuki Motocross bike, with tires that looked like a pair of black circular saws, was resting against the rear bumper of an old Ford Fiesta.

"It kind of looks like our first place," I said. "Same color brick. And the pitch of the roof line—"

Barks exploded from deep inside the house. It sounded like a convention of Rottweilers—loud enough so I could imagine the walls shaking. I thought I saw the curtains part a few inches in the middle of the picture window. When the dogs stopped raising hell, a wolf began howling.

"This is Waco waiting to happen." Elise had already picked up her bicycle and gotten back on. "*Allons-y.*"

§

A COUPLE OF WEEKS later, I was out riding when the sun was higher and hotter than I like. SwanSong trees aren't big enough yet to shade anything, so I checked for my passkey card—it was inside my Velcro security pocket—and followed the mailman when he drove out the main gate. There'd be cool shadows on any of the secondary roads, and maybe even a breeze coming down from the mountains. I pedaled behind the mailman on his route, something I'd never done before. With him pulling over for every RD box, I managed to keep up until he turned down the red clay road.

Since he had nothing to stop for now, he could make better time than I could. When he was about to pass me coming the other way, I flagged him down.

"Wanna race me, Gary?"

I wondered how he knew my name, until I realized that he'd been looking at my envelopes for the better part of a year now. Turned out he'd bought a Cornish Rex kitten from *Le Faux Roar*.

"Never grew much," he said. "But we love the little guy."

I asked him what he knew about the guy at the end of the road.

"He's a Gary, too. Gary Wood. Lives by himself now."

"What's he like?"

"Why don't you ask him?" The mailman grinned. "Oh, it's safe." He put his Jeep back into gear. "People up here just do things a little different."

§

"I GOT TO KEEP my mailbox secure," Gary Wood explains. He's re-locking his mailbox with one hand while he holds his Duke Power bill in the other. "Teenagers out here, they liable to do anything to your mailbox. Bust it with a baseball bat. Put a cherry bomb inside. Pull it up with a chain tied to a trailer hitch. They done it all."

"Why didn't you call the police?"

He rests his work shoe against the bottom of the metal cage. "This here's set in a foot of concrete, Mr. Michel. It ain't going nowhere."

"I can see that," I say.

His smile's like the eye of a needle turned sideways. I wonder how he lost all his teeth. "Let's take us inside," he says. "Get something to wet our whistles."

Today both of the boys are on the teeter-totter. He stops to pat their heads and check their air pressure. "You know the new area code?"

It isn't that new. "864," I say.

"That's right. But I never did no long distance. So I told my boys 803. My mistake. I learned them their home number before they could put two steps together. But if they far enough away, they ain't gonna get through to me. Not by no phone."

Inside the house, no dogs are in sight. While he pours us glasses of sweet tea, I squint at the cassette in his tape deck: *The Sounds of Halloween.*

"That's why I need the mailbox," he says from the kitchen. "Same address."

Laminated newspaper stories lie on the coffee table, like big place mats. CHILDREN DISAPPEAR. KIDS STILL MISSING. Finally, in smaller type, WHERE ARE THEY NOW?

He hands me my drink, but we don't sit down. "They make inflatable women, too. You know that? But it don't seem right for no playground." He takes off his cap the way men do when the national anthem is about to begin at a baseball game. "They was good boys, Mr. Michel. Every day I thank God for giving them to me as long as He did."

"I don't have any children," I say.

"I kept on racing. You can do some things with a motorsickle when you're not overly concerned." He smiles with his empty mouth. "That's why she left. But the po-lice, they thought Crystal went to be with the boys. That she planned the whole thing." He rattles the ice cubes in his glass, tilting it to get the last few drops of sweet tea into his mouth. "That's when I built it. I figured if she ever come back, she could see for herself I still had those boys in my heart."

We go back into the yard and sit with the kids on the teeter-totter. We put them into our laps, rock up-down, up-down. We even start laughing. From a distance, we must look like three generations of Southern manhood blessed by God. I haven't felt this much at home since we moved to SwanSong.

"I could use a car," I say. "But I'd have to keep it here. How much would you take for the Fiesta?"

"I can't sell it," he says. "That's Crystal's." Gary sits his end of the teeter-totter into the ground. He's squeezing his little boy so tight I can see the base of the valve bulging in his neck. "You need to drive anywhere, Mr. Michel, you give me a call." He recites his seven numbers and makes me repeat them, over and over, until he's certain I'll never forget.

Weather

I'D TUCKED MY PARAKEET in for the night and started emptying the dishwasher when I heard my husband shouting over the TV in the other room.

"HFC! HFC!"

I winced and didn't even bother to put down my linen towel on my way to his recliner. "I wish you wouldn't use that term, Noel Willis." I smiled, to take the visible edge off my annoyance. "It's blasphemous."

"C'mon, Hilda." He muted the TV sound. "It's just three letters."

"Yes," I said. "Like KKK."

"More like KFC." He sipped the red wine I'd brought him fifteen minutes ago, at the top of the eleven o'clock news. "We do saviors right."

I rolled my eyes, but before he could see them the station had come back from commercial break. "How dare they," he said, pointing to the fifty-inch screen.

I saw a spindly old woman, smiling like she was about to lose her dentures, gesticulating toward a digital representation of the upper atmosphere. "Hallowed be Thy name," I whispered. The mute button was still on, so I couldn't hear whether a break in the drought was in our Extended Outlook. "Whatever happened to our Weather Tootsie?"

§

THE NEXT MORNING, since Noel wasn't teaching summer school, we were having a late, luxurious breakfast on our little back porch. With the screens wide open, the air in Belladonna almost smelled sleepy. We were both still in our pajamas, which I'd just said were exactly the color of Dovie's feathers.

"Atlanta," Noel said. His voice came from behind the newspaper he was holding up like a soiled bedsheet. "Says here she went to Atlanta." He passed the Local News section across the table, barely clearing the butter dish, but at least now I could see his face. "Seems like our Weather Tootsie upgraded."

I continued reading the story aloud. *"Greenville is a nice place to begin your career,"* I intoned. *"Not a nice place to end it."*

We both laughed. We've been living in upstate South Carolina ever since we came to Clemson as teenagers.

"I'll miss her workplace-inappropriate attire," Noel said, wiping an imaginary tear from his eye with a real paper napkin.

Our Weather Tootsie had been a young Hispanic woman with impossibly smooth, radiant hair—even darker than mine used to be—framing her brilliant smile. The first time we'd seen her on WFOP, Noel said she must've spent all her off-camera hours with a peroxide rinse in her mouth. "Mammals don't have teeth that white," he'd declared. "It's not natural." Noel's taught high-school biology ever since he graduated from college, so he should know. But then, the rest of the Weather Tootsie probably wasn't entirely natural either.

"Her blouses *were* two sizes too small," I admitted, folding the newspaper so I could finish my whole wheat toast.

"She looked like a snake ready to shed her skin," Noel agreed. "But her replacement." He grimaced. "What'll we call her?"

I heard Dovie singing from her cage in the corner of the kitchen. I listened to the first eight notes of *Amazing Grace* before I said, "The woman looks like a big stork."

"She's too old to be carrying babies," Noel said. "Even in her beak. I bet she's even older than—"

He stopped himself. I didn't have to say anything.

"Than I am," he finally said. Noel took back the newspaper and held it horizontally this time, over his scrambled Egg Beaters. "Guess what? Her name's Christina Crane." Our gazes locked, and we both said the same three words aloud.

"The Weather Crane."

Things like that happen when you've been married to somebody for over thirty-seven years.

§

As June stretched into July, the drought got worse. Moderate became Severe, and Severe became Extreme. Georgia even tried to redraw its border so it could pump water directly from the Tennessee River to Atlanta. In upstate South Carolina, lawns began looking sparse and colorless as the Weather Crane's hair. Anderson County told people they couldn't wash their cars anymore, and in Greenville we couldn't remember when an outdoor burning ban hadn't been in effect.

After the Weather Tootsie's departure, we'd boycotted the eleven o'clock news, but as the drought deepened, we began watching again. All the lakes dropped to their lowest levels in recorded history. Every other night on the TV, you saw footage of Lake Hartwell with cracked mud at the end of already-extended docks, the only visible water puddling in the distance, like a mirage. Lake Keowee wasn't much better off. I wanted some tips about how we could help, what we could contribute, even though we'd been living in a Belladonna condo for the past three years and no longer owned a yard. "Hey," Noel said. "I'm contributing. I'm only flushing for *solid* biological waste."

Tonight, Christina Crane was wearing a pale pantsuit, so you couldn't quite tell where her blunt hair ended and her collar began. She hunched over, then started raising her unsteady hand. "Marginally cooler air is up to our north—" Now she began lowering her arm. "While even warmer air is down to our south." She stared straight into the camera. "Couldn't we all use a good Artic blast about now?"

"*Arctic*," Noel snickered. "Least she could do is learn the lingo."

"The Tootsie didn't know the lingo, either," I reminded him. "She called snow frozen percipitation."

When Noel raises his eyebrows, they move just like caterpillars. "I never noticed."

"You were too busy ogling her workplace-inappropriate attire."

"Why not? She looked like a pole dancer, for God's sake."

I felt the blood coming up in my face. For a year and a half, I took Senior Pole Dancing lessons from Mona Beegle as part of my weight-control program. But I never told Noel.

"She could melt the wax in *my* dissecting pan," he continued. "Any day of the—HFC!"

I refocused on the screen. The Weather Crane was kneeling in front of her telestrator, praying. Praying for rain that would bless the just and the unjust. I'd never seen that on TV before, except on Sunday mornings, before I head to church.

"Dear God." Noel folded his hands, melodramatically. "Grant us, in Your infinite wisdom, the second coming of Tootsie."

"The woman's just trying to help," I said.

"Bleep," Noel said. "Bleep. Bleep. Bleep."

"What's that?"

"My Super Doppler Fundar," Noel explained. "Idiocy must be in our Extended Outlook."

"Matthew 5:45 is *idiotic*?" I hadn't been this mad since Noel had insulted my minister while I was in the recovery room of the hospital, twenty years ago. The poor man was only trying to help me pray, but he made the mistake of grabbing my husband's hand as well as my own.

"What are you humming?" he demanded now.

"*The Thirsty Are Called to Their Lord*," I muttered. And I was.

§

EACH NIGHT, AFTER Noel began snoring, I began to pray. I'd get out of bed and shuffle into the bathroom, just to make sure he didn't wake up. Sometimes he did. Noel is a light sleeper. If he stirred, I'd just flush the toilet, then slip back under the covers, clasp my hands, and stare at the dark ceiling. But if his raspy breathing hadn't changed, I'd kneel next to my side of the bed—the moonlit side, by the east window—and whisper the gospel according to The Weather Crane: "Dear Lord in Heaven, send rain on the just and on the unjust. Bless us all with rain."

§

AFTER NOEL WENT back to teaching in late August, I started helping out with the Mosquito Ministry. Our—my—new pastor, Reverend Rogers, is a fitness fanatic eager to increase the size of his flock. *And decrease its average age.* So he goes to the Marsh Mellow Trail whenever the Xtreme Horizons Club has a scheduled excursion, and he sets up a table with bottled water and insect wipes. He doesn't preach, but he attaches our church bulletin to each bottle with a rubber band.

One morning, after the last hikers had left and we were packing things up to bring back to our Family Life Center, Reverend Rogers said, "I hear Noel's retiring soon."

I was surprised he even knew my husband's name. Noel never goes to church, and Reverend Rogers has only been here since Methodist Relocation Day in June. "Actually, he is retired. Technically. He's on the TERI plan, so he gets to draw his salary and his pension at the same time."

The Reverend lowered the box of water bottles into his trunk. "Sounds like a sweet deal."

"When he stops teaching, he'll've been at it for forty years." I laughed. "He calls it his forty years in the wilderness."

"Maybe I'll be seeing him," Reverend Rogers said. "When he has more free time."

A picture of my asking Noel to Sunday service popped into my head, and I wanted to get it out of there just as fast as I could. "Reverend, do you believe in the power of prayer?"

"If I don't, I'm in the wrong business."

"Have you been praying about the drought?"

He raised his eyebrows, just like Noel. "Have *you* been watching Christina Crane?" My face must have answered his question. "It's a tricky thing, Hilda. Weather isn't just a personal matter. When it rains, it rains on Little League baseball, roofers who don't get paid, highways that get too slick for an eighteen wheeler to—"

But I persisted. "Can God make it rain?"

"Yes," my minister finally said, running his fingers through his curly blond hair. "But He's been known to get a little carried away."

§

WE'D GOTTEN A few stray showers, but come September we were still officially at the dead center of Extreme Drought on the weather map—a red bull's-eye surrounded by orange and yellow that radiated into north Georgia, Tennessee, and both Carolinas. I'd started watching the late TV news in my sewing nook, with Dovie, to get away from Noel. Something about Christina Crane made him angry.

"Pray for rain. Pray for rain. From cumuloose clouds," he'd mocked. "You know that's what she calls them? Cumuloose clouds."

"You're just jealous," I'd said.

"Of what?"

"Well, she's on the TV." After he'd snickered, I said, "And she probably makes more money than you do."

"That's right," Noel said. "But I'm not jealous. I'm bitter."

"What's the difference?"

"If I were jealous, I'd want her salary *and* her job." His voice climbed an octave. "Praying for rain."

"It can't hurt," I said.

"Prayers can't change the weather, Hilda." Then his eyebrows started crawling up his forehead. "Are *you* praying for rain?"

"Well, it can't hurt," I said.

"I can't believe we're having this conversation," he said, and he left the room.

§

WHEN THE DROUGHT finally broke, with a big tropical depression coming up from the Gulf of Mexico, Dovie died. Noel had brought her home and surprised me, nineteen years ago. He said he'd bought her at Mall Mart, but I knew better. Our departing minister, Ebenezer Paulsen, had left her behind in a cage, outside the parsonage, for Noel to find on Relocation Day. By Christmas I'd taught Dovie to sing the first eight notes of *Amazing Grace* and *Faith of Our Fathers* and *Praise God from Whom All Blessings Flow*—well, whistle them, not the actual words, which would've sounded like a joke coming from a parakeet—and sometimes I'd sing along with her.

"Low atmospheric pressure," Noel said. "It correlates with myocardial infarctions."

"Is that supposed to make me feel better?"

He stood up to hug me, like I knew he would, and I cried into the front of his shirt. "I know you loved that damn bird," he whispered, stroking my hair, letting it linger beneath his fingertips. "I'm sorry, Hilda."

§

AFTER THE RAINS had moved east, I buried Dovie in an old Christmas cookie tin, my favorite—the one with the holly branches and the bright red berries, the one that seemed to be waiting for a nest. I waited until the Livengoods' lights had gone out before I found a spot under a real holly bush, outside our bedroom window, because technically we didn't own the land outside our condominium. I parted the pine bark mulch and dug a small hole in the softened red clay with the little spade I use for my house plants. When I came back inside, Christina Crane was announcing that she was leaving WFOP.

Noel clapped his hands, three times. "It is finished."

I almost dropped my trowel when Christina Crane said the Weather Tootsie would be taking her place next week. Of course, she didn't call her the Weather Tootsie.

§

"STATISTICALLY INEVITABLE," Noel pronounced at the breakfast table the next morning. "Every drought is an aberration. It has to rain eventually. Prayers or no prayers."

"In Japan, the crane is a symbol of good fortune."

Noel didn't seem to have heard me. "I know why the Tootsie's coming back!"

"Really," I said.

"I Googled her. Seems she's been out of work for the past month. Remember that day it hit 105? She was talking to the sports guy and didn't know she still had a live mic in front of her. Told him it might be too hot to—*fornicate* out there." My husband was grinning. "That's just a close paraphrase. It got on Ytube and she was gone the next day."

At times like these, I'm glad I'm computer illiterate. "Maybe Greenville *is* a good place to end your career."

"You know, the rain missed Atlanta," Noel said. "They're still trying to steal that river from Tennessee."

"Maybe they need Christina Crane. She certainly solved our problem."

"Don't push it," Noel said. "Pride cometh before a fall. Even in September."

And I had to agree. Noel is a good man. He didn't have to bring Dovie home on that day. He could've let her stay out there in that June sun. A lot of so-called Christians wouldn't have stopped their cars.

"Finally things are back to normal around here," Noel said, right before he pecked my cheek on his way to school. "About time."

Now I watch him through the window as he pulls out of our condo's three-car garage. Noel will make a great old man some day in the not-too-distant future, when he's forgotten about Frog Dodgeball, vandalized microscopes, and parents who call him an instrument of Satan. He'll be fun, and funny, and gentle, and maybe I'll even talk him into doing Moveable Feasts with me. He can drive, and I can deal with the Methodist elders who can't get to our church suppers anymore. We have a good Extended Outlook, even if he does call Reverend Rogers "Lord of the Flies." But there's something else. Something he can't mock out of me even if I wanted him to, and Lord knows I don't. I will grow old with it, too, just as I will grow old with him, and God will figure out a way to bless us both.

Dog Days

THE CHIHUAHUA, PERCHED six inches behind the property line, had been yapping, every three seconds, for the past half hour. My wife and I were finishing our Sunday brunch on the deck. From behind her big sunglasses she muttered, "How do you say shut the fuck up in Spanish?"

Our new neighbor is a young Hispanic woman who does the weather for a local TV station. "*Silencio*," I said. "More or less."

"*Silencio*!" she shouted, more or less toward the dog.

But instead of retreating, it crossed the line and stood next to our garden shed. "Her electric fence isn't working," I explained. "The battery on the receiving collar must be dead."

The tiny dog kept barking, thirty feet from us. It couldn't have been much bigger than a good-sized squirrel.

"*Silencio*, you son of a bitch!"

"I think it's a female dog," I said.

That was a mistake. A big mistake. "How would you know?" My wife took off her sunglasses, glared at me, and slipped her bare feet into her Crocs. Then she limped across the back lawn and turned on the spigot to the garden hose that she uses to water her perennial beds.

"Bitch of a bitch!" she screamed, and, with the full force of the water, pinned the dog to the side of the shed. When it fell onto its back, she came closer with the nozzle and zeroed in on its nose. "Bitch of a bitch!"

Now she adjusted the nozzle to Jet Stream and started pushing the little dog back toward the property line, still aiming toward its head. She didn't have to touch it, not even with her waterproof sandals. When she got it past the red training flags for the electric fence, she finally turned off the hose. The dog wasn't moving.

"The premises are secure," she smiled, baring the dentures she's worn ever since her teeth were knocked out and her knees broken, in our own home. Our former home. Then she returned our dishes and silverware to the bamboo serving tray and brought them back into the house we've been living in for the past ten years.

The dog still wasn't moving. But when I raised my eyes to our neighbor's master bedroom, I could have sworn the curtains parted. Of course, that was impossible, since our neighbor lived alone and she'd been double-shifting on Weekend Weather after her new job in Atlanta didn't work out last year, after she'd slunk back to her old one in South Carolina. Her salary couldn't amount to much, especially now. I wondered how she'd been able to buy into Belladonna—even one of the patio homes.

When she'd introduced herself to the neighborhood at the poolside picnic on the Fourth of July, she'd said she'd gotten a Chihuahua for protection. They were *pequeñas*, but they were good watch dogs. She'd used the feminine adjective, *pequeñas*, while she'd laughed and tossed back her long, glossy hair. Nobody had said anything. I remembered thinking she was the kind of woman who makes grown men speechless and their wives just as speechless, but for a very different reason. Then I saw those rippling curtains again, across her sliding glass door, and I figured the air conditioning must be coming up through her floor vent.

§

I KEPT HOPING the whole afternoon that the dog was just unconscious. That it would get up and trot, or at least stagger, back to its miniature igloo beneath the pyracantha. But it didn't.

We'd had a pet once, right after we'd moved to Belladonna—an orange Abyssinian cat named Peaches. During the winter it liked to snuggle up with me, tucking itself between my chin and the fringe of the comforter. One night, after my wife had gotten up to use the bathroom, it nested on her pillow before she could get back to bed. So she picked up the pillow, cat and all, and put it into the laundry room, inside the dryer. She didn't turn on the machine, of course, but she'd latched the metal door, just to teach it a good lesson.

When she came back in the morning, the cat had made a mess of everything. Number One and Number Two. I didn't know any of this at the time. I'd slept through the night, and I'd left for my office while it was still dark outside. I figured Peaches had gone out through the cat door. But when I got home that evening, my head spinning from corporate tax returns, my wife told me about the dryer and the cat. After I wondered aloud where Peaches was hiding, she said, "Peaches is no longer with us." I hoped she'd just taken her to the animal shelter, but I didn't ask for details. It was only a couple of months after her own accident, and I'd already figured out that Martha now regarded her own domestic tranquility as a divine right, or at least a minor form of divine justice.

But when I heard our neighbor's automatic garage door opening, I thought I owed the woman an explanation. I found an old blanket in the bedroom closet, went into the back yard, and wrapped up the dog. It was so little, so *pequeña*, that my arms could hardly tell the difference in weight. Then I brought it around to the front of her house, where I was planning to ring the doorbell. But instead I found my neighbor in a midriff-knotted blouse and denim cutoffs, getting ready to wash her Mini-Cooper in her driveway. The car must've been in her garage all day long.

I didn't know what to say, so I handed her her dog. Despite my wife, it didn't even look bruised. "I'm sorry," I finally stammered. "I found her outside. I'm sorry." That, I thought, was just true enough. As a tax accountant, I'm well aware of the difference between avoidance and evasion.

She put the dog down inside the huge Tuscan garage, picked a few blades of grass out of its front paws, and covered its muzzle with the blanket. Then she went back outside to pick up her hose. I almost ducked, but I caught myself in time. She smiled her TV smile at me and said, "You are good to bring her home."

Although the woman didn't seem to have much of an accent on WFOP, she sounded different in person. More ethnic. "It was no trouble."

"Your wife, she is the only one Maria would bark at. *Otro lado.*"

The other side. I took three years of Spanish in high school. "Dogs, they know."

I was afraid to ask her what they knew, so I merely nodded.

"But she was only a dog," the woman continued. "I can get another."

"I can pay—"

She shook her head and picked up a big sponge, squeezing its suds over the hood of her Mini-Cooper. "It must be hard. It must be very hard." She shrugged her dark hair behind her shoulders, so it wouldn't get wet while she leaned over. "Living with that *loca*." I watched her hips move, behind her denim cutoffs, while I listened to the squish and squeak of the sponge. I couldn't help myself.

§

Loca. She hadn't always been *loca*.

We'd married late, and we both had plenty of money, and we both loved to garden. So we bought a big house, a McMansion and then some, with three acres of land for us to play with. Out in the middle of nowhere, off Highway 11. We landscaped the hell out of that place—me with my lawn tractors and line trimmers, Martha with her tea roses and giant peonies and more annuals than I could name, or even count. We had underground irrigation, fieldstone terraces. A poolside cabana. For protection, I installed a security system, and I bought a gun. Our nearest neighbors were more than half a mile away.

One night, near the April 15 deadline, I was working late. Too late. By the time I got home from my office, the cop cars had turned our circular driveway into a light show, and Martha was already on her way to the hospital.

She'd given up on me and gone to bed, and she'd forgotten to set the alarm system, which was usually my job. When she'd heard the commotion downstairs—and the women's voices—she'd grabbed my gun and called the county police.

That's when one of them came into the bedroom, while she was still on the phone, and blinded her with a flashlight. Martha pointed the gun, and tried to pull the trigger. Nothing happened. The safety was still on.

Martha doesn't remember much after that. Only the nylon stocking over the burglar's face, only the gun being pulled out of her fingers. And the laugh—a woman's laugh—as the flashlight beat down on her own face, again and again and again. Her knees must have come later.

The burglars figured the cops were on their way, so they didn't have time to grab much. Just the jewelry in plain sight, including the big diamond solitaire and the wedding band on Martha's fingers. And the gun.

We never got anything back—although the insurance covered all of it, of course—and I never bought another gun. While Martha was still in the hospital, I put the house up for sale because I couldn't bear to take her back there. I never wanted her alone in that place again. Hell, I didn't want to be alone in that place again. Anywhere else, I told her. Anywhere else. Her choice. So we moved to Belladonna, the safest gated community on the planet, or at least in Greenville County, South Carolina. I wouldn't need my tractors anymore, so I sold them along with the house. But we'd still have a tiny yard for Martha to putter around in, once she got back on her feet.

§

August came and went. It's a slow month for me, so I do a lot of swimming. It keeps me in pretty good shape for a guy on the far side of fifty. On Labor Day, on my way to Belladonna's community pool, I met our neighbor, going in the opposite direction. Barefoot, in a bikini, she was walking a little dog that looked identical to her old one.

"Where is your wife?"

Even before her accident, Martha wouldn't be caught dead in a bathing suit. "She doesn't swim," I said.

"*Yo tambien*. Not today."

"They're pretty strict about the rules around here," I said. "You can't bring pets to the pool." I bent my knees to scratch behind the dog's ears. "Even this wittle baby. What's your name, wittle baby?"

She jerked the dog's choke collar, lifting its four feet clear from the sidewalk. It looked like it was treading water, twisting and whimpering, trying to get back to my extended hand. "She will be just like my first Maria." When I backed away, the woman returned the dog to the ground, to the same spot where I'd been scratching it. "*Pequeña.* But fierce."

§

When I returned home, after twenty laps in the big pool, Martha was sobbing in the sunroom. She was still in her gardening clothes. Speechless, she led me to the answering machine and played the message she'd found after she'd finished dead-heading her flowers.

Someone was thanking me. Thanking me for my compassion. For making her feel alive. For giving her my manhood that very afternoon. "Who is it?" Martha finally said. "Who have you been with?"

What could I say? I'd just walked down the street in my bathing trunks. "Martha, take a deep breath, okay? I've just been swimming. Swimming. You can smell the chlorine." I hugged her, to make my point. Her sobbing slowed down to a teary moan.

"Who is it, for God's sake?"

"I don't know, Martha." My chin was perched on her trembling shoulder, and I looked out the sunroom window into the backyard. "I don't know."

And I didn't know. But I had a pretty damn good idea.

§

That September, whenever I was late from work, there'd be a call. From a blocked number. If Martha answered, the phone would go dead. But if she let it ring, there'd be a message, for me, for Clayton, always similar, but never the same. Thanking me, hinting at intimacy but never saying anything specific about times, or places, or means of gratification. I tried not to be late, but in my business that's not easy. Clients will walk in at quarter to five, on their own way home from work, with letters from their investment brokers or the IRS, and they'll want their answers right away. They're worried. We're in the middle of The Great Recession. You can't blame them.

We thought about disconnecting the machine, or changing our number, but it's the one my clients have been using in emergencies for years. We reprogrammed the message with Martha's voice instead of my own, but it didn't make any difference. The woman kept calling.

One Saturday evening, I was watching Notre Dame football on TV when Martha came home from the Econoclast, from her weekly shop. "How could you, Clayton!" she screamed. "How could you?" She was holding the blanket that I'd used when I'd taken back the first Chihuahua. That's when I remembered it was the one we'd used for picnics, before we were married.

"That's it," I said. I didn't even bother to grab a coat, even though it was damn close to freezing, and I ran straight over to our neighbor's house. When I rang the bell, the new dog started barking. It wouldn't stop, and I wouldn't stop. After a couple of minutes, the woman finally answered the door, and I walked inside.

No furniture anywhere, a bare room with nothing but drapes.

"I hope you're moving out," I said. "That would be a good idea."

"You've been talking with your *loca*," she smiled. She was holding the dog in her arms, against her red bathrobe. "It shows."

"What did you tell her?"

"*La verdad*," she said. "That is about to happen." She tossed the dog, underhand, in my direction. Without thinking, I caught it, then lowered it to the hardwood floor. It seemed unsurprised, as if it had been rehearsing for this all afternoon, and even licked my hand. When the dog followed the woman toward the back of the house, I followed the dog.

We both stopped at the end of the hallway. The woman was standing at her bedroom window, with her robe puddled on the floor behind her.

She had nothing on. Nothing.

The curtains on the sliding glass door were fully open, and she was facing outside. Toward my house. I could see Martha at our kitchen window, her hand over her mouth.

Now the woman turned off the overhead light, and she walked toward me. "Your *loca* killed my dog." She held her open palms toward me, the red running down from her wrists, then sank to her knees.

I ran for the robe, to get something to stop the bleeding. That's when she turned the light back on, and I looked at Martha, and then at my own two hands.

§

SHE HADN'T SLASHED her wrists. She'd used nail polish, which I hadn't seen in the living room, since the robe was red and had oversized sleeves. She laughed when I bent over to help her, and she even kissed her lipstick onto the front of my shirt.

"What the hell are you, anyway?"

"A *loca*. Just like your wife." Now she broke into Broadcaster's English. "But I can speak Anglo for you, Clayton. I'll just pretend my nose is in my mouth. Do you like that better?"

I wasn't looking at her nose, or her mouth. Her breasts were poised and perfect, staring straight at me. She was still naked, the most beautiful woman I'd ever seen that way. In the flesh. I was still holding her robe. So I wrapped up the dog, and I walked, backwards, very slowly, back down the hallway.

"Take it home!" she shouted. "For your *loca*!"

And I would. I'd tell Martha I'd rescued it. I'd explain everything. I'd show her the nail polish that had passed for blood in that dark hallway, nail polish that she could peel with her own fingers off the nubs of that terrycloth robe. I'd tell her we'd keep the dog, and we'd name it together, and we'd build a fence, a real one, out back, and when she asked me how high, I'd tell her, "Whatever it takes." She'd believe me. I knew she'd believe me. We've been through worse than this already. But just to be sure, I took the little dog's rear end and rubbed it into that red blotch on my shirt, until it was the dull, ugly color of the truth.

Treenapping

THE HUSBAND WAS LESLIE and the wife was Lou. Lou Strubb. "Short for Louise," she said, smiling and shaking my hand like Mary Tyler Moore on steroids. Leslie was just short, bald as a football helmet with a skinny mustache over his lip. He could've been one of those overpaid midgets who say things like *I keeck a touchdown.*

They led me into a sixty-eight-degree living room about the size of the Hyatt Regency, full of skylights and potted plants. My shirt was still dripping like a dishrag from the triple-digit afternoon outside. That's what I like about Belladonna Security work—it lets you see how lucky you really are.

"I understand you folks had a B and E."

Lou poured me a cup of coffee from a silver urn. I guess she'd given her maid a half day off. "Not exactly, Sergeant Blessington. They didn't violate our residence. Just our property."

The coffee must have been left over from breakfast—room temperature and blacker than asphalt. "Ma'am, what did they take?"

"My *Acer palmatum.*"

I handed her my pencil and pad. I'm not the world's greatest speller.

"A dwarf Japanese maple," Lou explained. "They tore it right out of the ground."

Leslie said something about the bloody people who live in the Piedmont—which I didn't appreciate, since I'm upstate Carolina born and bred. He was sitting on a leather recliner in the next time zone, holding up a big black notebook named PARADISE LOST. "You should have called the congressman, Lou."

"I *did* get him elected," Lou said. "Sugar?"

I told her no thanks. "Estimated value?"

"Of the tree?" Lou was stirring her own drink, which definitely wasn't coffee. "It's priceless. A gift from my father. But I suppose you could buy one of similar size for, oh—five thousand dollars."

"Five *hundred*, dear," Leslie said. "The Almighty Father was never *that* generous."

"Forgive my husband," she said. "Leslie doesn't know anything about trees. A perfect *Acer palmatum* with a six inch diameter trunk and a six foot circular crown. Ask Doris."

Doris is my wife. She's the gardening columnist for the local paper, or at least what's left of it. She used to work out of the newsroom, and when that disappeared she worked out of our house—until we sold it to put our two girls through college. Now she emails her stories from a no-frills condo in the middle of nowhere, which we've nicknamed The Empty Nest Egg.

"We suspect gang violence," Lou said. "Our mailbox was destroyed in 1989, you know. Have you reviewed the file?"

She freshened my coffee while I ground my teeth. "That was twenty years ago, ma'am. And teenagers aren't much interested in trees they can't roll with toilet paper."

"Then what are we dealing with? International terrorists?"

She hadn't stopped stretching her mouth since I'd arrived. I tried to outsmile her, which seemed like a good idea at the time. "Ma'am, have you thought about getting some motion detectors for your yard?"

"We've considered it," Lou said, folding her hands in her lap. "But we've decided we want a stakeout."

"*She* wants a stakeout." The voice came from behind PARADISE LOST. "*I* want to call the congressman."

I spoke to Lou. "Well, I'd try the motion detectors first. They'd be less expensive than a private investigator."

"We'd feel more secure," Lou said, "with a *uniformed* officer."

My own uniform began to itch. "Mrs. Strubb—"

"Lou," she said.

"Lou," I said. "This boy might not come back for three months. He might could never come back. Last time I counted, there were

487 domiciles in Belladonna. We can't tie up one of our men on a permanent basis to protect your shrubbery."

"Speak with your captain, Sergeant Blessington. That's all I ask."

I stood up and straightened my holster. "Consider it done."

An enormous calico cat was licking her rump at the front door, and I didn't have room to step over her. "Perhaps you can help us with another problem," Lou said, pressing a hundred dollar bill into my palm.

I figured she was just testing me, so I put Ben Franklin into a statue with a big navel that let you see the wall behind it. "Ma'am, I'm not allowed to accept gratuities."

"This is an unofficial matter." She smiled at the cat until it whimpered and crawled downstairs. "Sometimes the most relevant part of our person is a bitsy bit *outside* the Boodaloo." Now Lou was rattling the ice cubes in her umbrella drink. "Do you have any suggestions? For keeping her little tushie in line?"

Just when you think you've seen it all, they show you something else. "Ma'am, I'm afraid I don't have the authority."

"Of course," she said. "I understand completely. But do say hello to Doris on my behalf. Tell her I *adore* her philosophy of organic pest control!"

§

CAPTAIN BILL MAZZARELLI was eating a tuna fish sandwich at his desk when I got back to the Belladonna Security Station. He saw me through the glass door and motioned me inside his office. "You want halfa this, Sandy? I can't handle it."

"Okay," I said. "What's the joke?"

"No joke. It's *good* tuna fish." He took another bite. "No Charlies for Captain Bill!"

"The Strubbs," I said.

"Abducted tree." Captain Bill licked his teeth clean so he could speak with more conviction. "You're the most qualified officer to investigate a felony outsida the animal kingdom."

"I'll fill out the 23-A," I said. "Just don't do me any more favors."

Now he was wiping his fingers on his desk calendar. "I heard about these guys on Long Guyland." Captain Bill came to us from Manhattan South. Put in his papers so he could draw his New York City pension and work on his golf game twelve months a year. Belladonna lets him play for free. "Treenappers. They go after firewood while people are on vacation. Trying to turn Suffolk County into an effing tank trap. Could happen here," he said, balling up the Saran Wrap from his sandwich and shooting it at the wastebasket. He missed. "Maybe it's a Mafia franchise, you know? Like McDonald's. If we don't catch them oily—"

I cleared my throat. "For your information, Captain, the Strubbs lost an *Acer palmatum*. No firewood value." Then I picked up the plastic and slam-dunked it into the can. "They want us to stake out the place."

"Sounds good to me," Captain Bill said. "I'll put you on the duty roster for tonight."

I stared straight at him. "This is Monday night."

Captain Bill slid open his desk drawer and took out a computer spreadsheet. It was the roll of honor for the Belladonna Friends of Order. To keep property assessments down, we depend a lot on voluntary contributions.

"One hundred percent confidential," Captain Bill said. "I didn't show you this."

There were more Cherubs and Angels and Archangels than you could shake a stick at, but only two Guardian Angels on the list: Mrs. and Mr. Lou Strubb.

"They been real good to us," Captain Bill said, patting me on the shoulder. He was trying to Relate. "Go home and get some sleep, Sandy. You deserve it."

"Sure, Captain," I said.

"And say hello to Doris for me."

"Sure, Captain," I said. I don't like to Relate. Especially in September. Especially on Monday night.

§

THE STRUBBS' 1948 Lincoln Continental had Corinthian upholstery. I sat behind the steering wheel, trying to look inconspicuous. But I opened the driver's window for some fresh air when Lou went back inside the house at 10:30 p.m.

I was surprised to hear so many crickets singing on the lawn. You'd think they'd hunker themselves down in honeysuckle or ivy, but vacant lots in Belladonna are hard to come by, even for insects. Everything was manicured to death.

That was a thought. I imagined a torturer yanking off fingernails, one by one, then painting the wounds with nail polish. You do strange things on a stakeout to stay awake. I wanted to turn on the radio, but that would have been unprofessional. So I amused myself by making up new lyrics to old songs and singing them in my head. My best one was from the Beatles.

One day you'll look
To see I've gone
If the Packers are playing
I'll swallow my gun.

So much for my mood. It was past midnight, but some of those squat candles you see in churches were still flickering in the windowsill of the Strubbs' master bedroom suite. There I was, sitting in an antique car that could double my net worth, while Lou and Leslie were sipping some hundred dollar wine I couldn't even pronounce, let alone spell, and playing Floozie in the Jacuzzi. . . .

I must have dreamt that. I didn't even know if they *had* a Jacuzzi. The next thing I remember was Lou standing next to the side view mirror, tapping the bridge of my glasses at dawn.

"Look," she said, pointing to a little stump next to the hand-painted mailbox at the bottom of their terrazzo driveway.

A three-by-five card fell off my lap before I could swing my legs out of the Lincoln.

THEY ALSO SERVE WHO ONLY SIT AND WAIT.

"Milton wrote that," Leslie said. "*John* Milton."

When I asked for Mr. Milton's address, Leslie tightened the belt of his bathrobe and leaned into his car. "It's from a poem," he said. His morning breath was hitting me flat in the face. "Obviously our perpetrator knows my reading preferences."

Lou was already down by the roadside, motioning us to join her. She'd found a strange garbage bag by the curb. It was filled with chopstick sized branches and dark green leaves.

"Before, it was merely abduction," she whispered. "Now, it's murder."

§

IT WAS WORSE THAN murder—now, it was personal. I used to be a real cop. Greenville County Northwest Area Command. I don't like being embarrassed by some sonnet-sniveling bozo with garden shears and a Glad bag. I went straight to the condo and told Doris what had happened—except for me falling asleep in the Lincoln. She was already working on tomorrow's column at her computer.

"How rich are they?"

"Very," I said. "Especially by our standards." We're semi-retired, but we still have three more years before our Social Security can kick in, even at 75%. Not to mention six more years before Medicare.

"Then all they need is a plant," she said.

I asked her what kind.

"A ploy. A ruse. This yard boy's a local, whoever he is. He *has* to read my column." She swiveled around in her task chair and grinned. "The trouble with you, Sandy, is you've stopped watching television."

She got that right. "Not by choice."

"He knows you're looking for him now. But we might could tempt him with something exotic. Something just too sexy to pass up." She took down a reference book from the shelf above her desk. Her forehead puckered up as she leafed through the index. I've always envied Doris's powers of concentration. She graduated technical college, top of her class. She wouldn't have noticed a tornado, unless it blew her book open to the wrong page. "Bingo," she said.

I read the words as they came up on her monitor.

Ben Franklin Comes to Belladonna

The historic *Franklinia alatamaha* was discovered along the banks of the Alatamaha River by botanist John Bartram in 1765. Named for Benjamin Franklin, the *Franklinia* was last seen in the wild around 1790 and is officially the rarest native ornamental in the world.

This deciduous flowering shrub has 4–6 inch oblong leaves that are lime to emerald green in summer, changing in fall to exquisite shades of burgundy. The spectacular 2–3 inch snow-white five-petalled flowers with gold stamens appear from mid-July until frost. The candelabra-type branching, striped bark, and fissured trunk make *Franklinia* a year-round treat.

Lou and Leslie Strubb of Belladonna have recently purchased the finest specimen in the Southeast from Plantadise Nursery. Enjoy viewing this beautiful ornamental at 113 Arbor Drive.

"Perfect," I said. "Print it." I punched the Strubbs' number and got their answering machine, but Lou picked up as soon as she heard my voice.

"I've always wanted a *Franklinia*," she said. "I'll call Plantadise right away."

"We're gonna bury this boy," I said. "He's gonna wish he'd never seen a shovel."

§

THE *Franklinia* WAS DELIVERED Wednesday morning, Doris's article came out in the afternoon paper, and I was back on stakeout Wednesday night. Whoever that boy was, he wouldn't catch me sleeping again in the Lincoln—although Lou had left it out in the driveway as a decoy. At dusk I'd walked all the way from the Security Station and sat in a pack of marble statues at the center of the Strubbs' front yard. I put my chin on my right hand and tried to look as Greek as possible.

Like me, he didn't drive. He came at around 3:30 a.m., with a shovel and a flashlight that had a red filter over the lens. He propped the light against the trunk of that staked *Franklinia*. Then he started to dig.

I waited until he'd begun using the handle of his shovel like a crowbar. That's when I came to life, without making a sound.

Except for my Reeboks, I was in full uniform. I didn't want him questioning my authority and doing something foolish. I'd spent twenty years on the job without firing my weapon, and I wanted to keep it that way. So I drew my service revolver and came up alongside him. He was wearing an old George W. Bush mask and a warmup suit.

"Make a move, Mr. President, and you're dead wood. This is Belladonna Security."

He stopped digging but didn't say a word.

"Mission accomplished," I said. "Drop the shovel."

He pushed it away from his waistband. It missed the *Franklinia* and hit the ground, handle first.

"Good decision," I said. "Now turn around and slide that shovel to me with your left foot. Keep your hands where I can see them."

He did it. I picked up the shovel and the flashlight, then pointed over to a medium sized pin oak. I tapped on the bark with the barrel of my service revolver.

"You like trees," I said. "Hug it."

He put his arms around the trunk until his fingers joined on the other side. After I'd cuffed his wrists, I walked toward the house to tell the Strubbs.

"Congratulations!" Lou's voice was coming from underneath the chassis of the Lincoln. She must've been laying there all night, checking up on me.

"I got him," I said.

Lou crawled out past the front wheels and used the chrome bumper to pull herself up to her feet. "Let's go see the perp," she said.

I removed the red filter from the flashlight and shined it into the two small holes at the front of Dubya's head.

"Payback time!" Lou shouted. She grabbed the floppy latex ears and pulled.

It was Leslie.

"You little devil," she giggled, right over the top of her smile. "You tricked me!"

"Outstanding police work!" he said, stretching that little mustache of his up into a straight line. "For once, my property assessment hasn't been taken in vain!"

"Where are the keys?" Lou said. "I'll drive us all to the Security Station!"

Leslie couldn't raise his arms, but he mumbled something about his sinister pocket. Then he called her his sovereign mistress and empress of this fair world. He sounded like he was somebody used to being forcibly restrained.

While Lou brought the Lincoln to the bottom of the driveway, I uncuffed Leslie and led him to the curb. Lou got out of the car and wiped the considerable shine off her husband's head with a lace handkerchief. "This should be as *genuine* as possible," she said. "Sergeant Blessington will have to sit between us."

"*After* he reads me my rights," Leslie said.

I did. After I excused myself to fill out the incident report, I unloaded my gun and put it back in my holster—just in case the Strubbs demanded more of my services. Somehow, it made me feel more secure.

And then the three of us scrunched up in the Lincoln together, shoulder to shoulder to shoulder, on the front bench seat.

"Do we need the air conditioner?" Lou whispered. It was pitch black in the car but I could feel her teeth shining right through me.

"Myself am Hell!" Leslie shouted.

"My husband used to teach college," Lou explained. "Until I married him."

Now he started fanning himself with Dubya's rubber face. "Me miserable!"

Well, that made two of us.

Breaking News

MA'AM, I KNOW IT AIN'T none of my business, but how'd you get your job with the TV? You go to college? All four years? In New Mexico? I guess it don't hurt none to look like no model, neither.

What was me and Dan Rather and Tom Brokaw doing at Wurst Case Scenario on a Monday afternoon? Well, I been fixing Mr. Scenario's motorsickle for several years now. We go way back to when I was racing dirt track. But today I was returning the weed wacker he uses to trim around his Portasigns in the parking lot. Needed a new spark plug and the carburetor flushed out. I figured I'd get me and my boys an early supper at the same time. Mr. Scenario always gifts me with a free meal every time I do work for him. Don't fool around with no checks, neither. Pays me hard cash, right on delivery. Wish I had more customers like him. Gave my boys two big helium hot dog balloons on their birthdays. Had their names hand-painted right under the name of his restaurant.

WURST CASE SCENARIO
Dan Rather
WURST CASE SCENARIO
Tom Brokaw

When we come in, I don't see Mr. Scenario, who usually does Mondays hisself cause it's a slow day. What I do see behind the counter is Barack Obama, but since it's almost Halloween, I figure he's just starting to celebrate early. He's fat, and he's short, and when he turns around to pick up some keys I see his neck's about three shades too white to be the real thing. I ask if I can see Mr. Scenario and he says Mr. Scenario isn't available at the moment. He says he thinks Mr. Scenario is gone for the day. I told him that was mighty strange, considering I told Mr. Scenario I'd be coming around at four thirty and this was precisely it. Four thirty. I told him Mr. Scenario never could take a day off in his life and Barack Obama just says, "Yes he can."

Then I heard something from inside the Bun Closet next to the grease pit. "You heared that?" I say. "Heared what?" Barack Obama says. I point to the Bun Closet and he tells me it's just the air conditioner cutting on and off cause it's been confused today, what with the weather front coming through. I say I believe I can fix that so he finds the right key and lets me in there. When I turn on the light I see Mr. Scenario next to the compressor, under a big pallet of Sara Lee Gourmets, with his legs sticking out and banging around like two wieners fell outta the buns. When I run over to help him, Barack Obama tells me this looks like a teachable moment, and he locks me up in there with Mr. Scenario.

And my boys are still out next to the drink station, getting a head start on their free meal.

The door to the Bun Closet's worse than sigodlin, so I can see out between the edge and the jamb right good. Thank the Lord for carpenters who don't know what in the world they're doing. I start yelling for my boys, and they run over to see if they can get me out, which they can't, and while they're trying, the first thing Barack Obama does is lock the front door of Wurst Case Scenario from the inside. Which is his big mistake. You never lock yourself *in* with Dan Rather and Tom Brokaw. You got a lick of sense, you lock yourself *out* with Dan Rather and Tom Brokaw. They're good boys but they're all boy, if you know what I mean. The President don't know what he's in for.

But then he takes this big gun out from under his black windbreaker and tells them both to lay down on the floor while he empties the register—they sell lottery tickets here, so it's more than just hot dog money we're talking about. I'm just about ready to mess my shorts. I'm just about ready to start rattling that sorry ass door and tell my boys to mind Mister Obama and treat him like the President he is when Dan Rather laughs and says that ain't no real gun, that's just a T68 paintball pistol with a ten-round magazine. And he runs up at him and jumps on his back.

They start twisting in circles around the drink station, and Dan Rather's hanging on, yelling "Courage! Courage! Courage!" He heared that on the internet when I was giving him his English lessons. Barack Obama's bucking hisself over that tile floor, like the most sorry ass bull you ever seen, trying to shake him off. When Dan Rather starts getting his fingers underneath the mask, Mister Obama drops the pistol so he can keep his face on for the foreseeable future. Meanwhile, little Tom Brokaw has run to the nearest table and got hisself a squeeze bottle of Kick Ass Jalapeno Hot Sauce. He hands it up to Dan Rather, who squirts it straight into the eyeholes, just before he jumps off of the President's back.

Next thing you know, Barack Obama starts screaming and ripping hisself off. Now he looks more like Adolph Hitler, with this black mustache about the size of a squashed horsefly—and he runs into the rest room, screaming his eyes out, where I can hear him turning on the faucet to get the Kick Ass off of his face. Dan Rather gets the master key Adolph left on the counter and lets me and Mr. Scenario outta the Bun Closet, and when we all run over to the rest room, Adolph is still trying to flush hisself out over the sink. Meanwhile Tom Brokaw has picked up the T68 and he slides past us and says, "That's nightly news for tonight!" while he empties the whole ten-round magazine into the back of that windbreaker. Just like he was a member of The Greatest Generation. Ma'am, that black jacket done turn just as red as your dress. Looks like somebody slaughtered a German hog on top of it. Now if Adolph manages to get hisself outta the store the po-lice won't have no trouble picking him outta the crowd on North Pleasantburg Drive.

Mr. Scenario calls I-C-CRIME and five cars get here in about three minutes. Good thing they know the way. If they'd've taken much longer, I think I might've got that weed wacker outta my truck and done me some indoor landscaping. Know what I mean? Maybe called up my big brother Melvin to borrow me one of his chain saws—so I could limb something up a little. But when I heared all of them sireens I just got Mr. Scenario's money outta Hitler's pockets and I kicked him in the nuts.

Can I say that on the TV?

No, I done give Mr. Scenario all the money. Then he said me and my boys can have Yellow Dog Democrats any day of the week, for the rest of our lives. Foot-longs with chili and slaw and mustard slathered over the top. Free drinks too. But Dan Rather got to be careful. He takes his sweet tea through a straw so he don't mess up his smile for his future career. That boy drinks up a storm, let me tell you. Tom Brokaw, he's partial to Diet Sprite so he got no problem.

Anyhoo, we won't need a nickel in Wurst Case Scenario from this day forward.

That's what Mr. Scenario said. And he is a man of his word.

No ma'am, I didn't raise Dan Rather and Tom Brokaw up to be no heroes. I just wanted them to talk good. When Crystal hid those boys they weren't much more than babies. Tom Brokaw didn't hardly know three words to string together. She took them off someplace and said they'd been kidnapped and even to this day I don't know where. We both went to the po-lice, and she cried and cried and cried. Then she ran herself away three weeks later. It was all over the newspapers. I still got them stories at home. Laminated every one. That's when I put them inflatable boys in my front yard, just to keep me company. Built me a playground, with a slide and a swing set and a big plastic worm, and started them off on either end of the teeter-totter in front of my picture window. I been looking at inflatable boys for seven years, just to remind me of my real ones. I done never give up. Not for one minute.

This June, Crystal brought them back in the middle of the night. It had to be Crystal. When I woke up on Father's Day, Dan Rather and Tom Brokaw was on the teeter-totter, with their names stapled onto their shirts, which I guess was Crystal's idea of being responsible. Them inflatables was stuck with a stick and lying on the ground like them chalk outlines you see on *CSI* after the bodies been carried to the morgue. Which didn't faze me none cause I didn't need them no more. I had my boys back. I'd been keeping Crystal's Ford Fiesta in the carport, all ready for her, just in case she ever come home. And now it was gone.

My best guess is she run off with Señor Wrap Number Two. Cause Crystal always was partial to his takeout and he disappeared right after she did. And them boys wasn't speaking nothing but

Spanish when I tried to hug them on the day they come back. Crystal ain't stupid, even if she did spell my name wrong on one of her tattoos. *Gary* don't got no *E*. Maybe she went south of the border for a while, till Señor Wrap Number Two finally told her Dan Rather and Tom Brokaw was just too much boy.

I just about got them all the way back to English now. Been working on them since June. We been watching all the old news on the internet, so they can learn to speak good. Boys got to have positive role models. You know that, right? That's why I named them Dan Rather and Tom Brokaw in the first place.

Little Tom just turned nine and his big brother's eleven. I drive them boys to school every day in my F-150 and they're getting A's in everything. English included! After all they been through.

Don't you believe a man ought to honor his responsibilities? I do. When they come back, I quit racing motorsickles and just kept on fixing them instead. Expanded myself to lawnmowers and weed wackers and chain saws and whatever else got a two-cycle engine. My friend Mr. Michel helped me set up my business proper. He even come up with a name. *Gary Wood Repair Anything*. I earn good, honest money. Pay my taxes on every check I get.

Don't you usually do us the weather on *NewsCenter Now* at eleven o'clock? You trying to branch out? Coming in early? Special assignment? You know, you talk real good for a Mexican lady. No offense. French and Eyetalian too? Good Lord. Maybe you know somebody could teach my boys how to speak Fartsi, so they can get themselves over there to the Middle East when they graduate high school. Get themselves in bedded, just like that Richard Mangle. Hell of a lot of future in that.

They got some talent. Come on over here, boys. Don't be shy. Let the weather lady take a listen to you. Tom Brokaw Wood, put down that T68. Dan Rather, hold up that hot sauce like it was a live mic. Speak good, just like I learned you at home. Come on now, boys. I bet even your momma and Señor Wrap still watch the news.

The Eye of the Needle

REVEREND ROGER ROGERS had serious reservations about the Faster Pastor Challenge.

On Maundy Thursday, when the WFOP station manager had called to ask for his commitment to a Fourth of July fundraiser, he'd heartily agreed. Roger had recently read about a Faster Pastor event in Colorado that had generated more than $50,000 for malaria prevention programs in Sub-Saharan Africa. He imagined potential synergy with the Mosquito Ministry he'd started on the local Marsh Mellow hiking trail a couple of summers ago—to impede the spread of the West Nile virus in upstate South Carolina. (He'd distributed water bottles, church bulletins, and insect wipes to profusely perspiring walkers, runners, and cyclists every Saturday.) Although he was an avid jogger and could finish a mile in just over five minutes, he'd never entered a competitive race. The Faster Pastor Challenge could show his congregation at Belladonna Methodist a side of his personality they'd never seen before—*and* encourage them to accord his Least of These Latin American Relief Fund the fundraising priority it deserved. Churches like his, enshrined in gated communities, had a way of being short sighted. Roger strongly suspected they'd hired him mainly for his youthful appearance and for his eminently memorable name.

But when the posters for the event came out on Mother's Day weekend, he was dismayed to discover that the Faster Pastor Challenge would take place not at the running track of the local college but at the Dark Corner Speedway. The picture he'd emailed to the TV station had been Photoshopped to include a flame retardant racing suit in place of his pulpit robe. His name topped the list of a dozen ministers—and Roger would be driving the *Jesus of Malibu* 888 car. How did they know he'd been raised on the coast of Southern California and owned a Chevrolet?

After the 11:00 a.m. Sunday service, while he was accepting smirks and backslaps and heartfelt good wishes from his flock in the narthex, he asked Hilda Willis if he could speak with her in his office. Hilda had been on Church Council at Belladonna Methodist for thirty-five consecutive years—longer than Reverend Rogers had lived in his earthly body. After he walked behind his desk and invited her to sit down in front of it, he briefly explained his misunderstanding with WFOP. Then he asked for her best wisdom on the matter. He was hoping she knew the station manager—Hilda had done so much work at soup kitchens and flower bulb fundraisers and charity concerts that she knew practically everybody in Greenville County—and he was hoping she could suggest a graceful way for him to withdraw from the upcoming event.

But Hilda thought the Faster Pastor Challenge was a wonderful idea—even better than the Mosquito Ministry, which had brought at least ten new families into the congregation. "It'll reach out to people we've never been able to touch before. Dirt track racing is like a second religion down here. Why, I bet even Noel will come out for the Faster Pastor!" Noel Willis, Hilda's husband, was a retired biology teacher who made only token appearances at Belladonna Methodist on Christmas Eve and Easter Sunday. "He told me this morning he thought you'd look cute in a helmet."

Reverend Rogers winced. He hated to put anything on his head that might disturb his curly blond hair.

"I'll take care of the publicity," Hilda promised. "You won't have to worry about a thing."

As always, Hilda was as good as her word. On Monday she called WFOP and discovered that admission would be twenty dollars—ten dollars for kids accompanied by their parents—and that each congregation would be responsible for selling its own tickets. Half the money would go to the church, and the other half would go to the winner of the Faster Pastor Challenge. Ministers would be driving their own vehicles, she assured him, but the format of the race would remain a secret until Independence Day.

The Eye of the Needle

§

For several weeks Reverend Rogers had been praying for a rain worthy of Noah, but the Fourth of July dawned like an outtake from Genesis 2:5. While he was finishing his chamomile tea, he watched the morning dew resurrect itself from the parsonage lawn and disappear into a cloudless sky. He heard himself sigh deeply. At times like these, he wished he were married—especially to somebody with a valid driver's license and with no reservations about making an absolute fool of herself in public. He zipped himself into the flame resistant Nomex racing suit that Hilda's Sunday School class had purchased for him without his knowledge, and he walked out to his car. At least he'd remembered to remove that rusty roof-mounted surfboard rack the day before.

He arrived at the Dark Corner Speedway at noon, parked his old Chevrolet on the infield, and milled around in the shade with the other ministers—while the teenagers from each congregation decorated the cars with self-adhesive vinyl numbers, fluorescent crosses, and door names like *Speed Demon* or *Fiendcatcher*.

"How come *you* get 888, *Jesus of Malibu*?" the minister from Evangelical Lutheran pouted at him, playfully. Her name was Angelina, as in Jolie. Mercifully, he'd forgotten her last name. A couple of months after he'd arrived in South Carolina, he'd sat next to her at an interfaith luncheon on social justice. When she raised her salad fork with her ringless left hand, his intestines had done an impromptu backflip. He'd just begun thinking of himself as a bachelor again. After he'd accepted his Belladonna appointment, his longtime girlfriend had decided she'd be better off staying in Claremont, California, pursuing a PhD in Practical Theology. She was no longer returning his calls. So he stammered out a dinner invitation while he was walking Angelina to her car—a pink Ford Mustang, he painfully remembered. She'd patted his shoulder, stretched her full lips into a kindly smile, and told him she was a lesbian.

Dr. Stan Dammers from Belladonna Primitive Baptist already had his helmet on. "Well, here's our poster boy!" He looked like an oversized Darth Vader, but his voice was a high, piercing tenor. "Now let's see if he can live up to his billin'."

"What are you driving?" Reverend Rogers asked. Even in the grandstand's shadow, he was starting to sweat inside his ridiculous suit.

"An Alianthus 780 ALI convertible," Dr. Stan squeaked, through his plexiglass visor.

"God is good," Reverend Angelina said. "That car goes for at least 90K."

"Save it for the straightaway, darlin'. I'm out to win this sucker." Dr. Stan swaggered across the track to inspect his car, *The Serpent Handler*.

"Better stay out of his way," the Presbyterian minister whispered, wiping the wide, wrinkled brow beneath his snowy hair. "He used to do this for a living."

§

BY 2:00 P.M. the grandstand was overflowing and the weekend anchor from WFOP had descended to the track, where he was belting out the national anthem into a battery powered microphone. Next to him stood a moped with 666 stenciled on its side. A black body suit crowned by a helmet sporting fiery twin horns hunched over the handlebars.

"The rules of the Faster Pastor Challenge are simple. Behold!" He gestured toward the moped rider, who obligingly revved up an unmuffled engine while the crowd booed. "Satan will get a sixty-six yard head start astride *The Inferno*, which has a top speed of thirty miles per hour. Each one of our Faster Pastors—"

The assembled congregations cheered, and the line of pastors waved to the grandstand.

"Each one of our Faster Pastors, in turn, will be—dare I say it?—in hot pursuit. The ordained driver must pass Satan before proceeding through the Eye of the Needle at the finish line. And yes, our needle is indeed in a haystack!" He pointed to a barrier of big rectangular bales lined up across the track, with a communion-table-sized gap in the middle. "If more than one of our twelve Holy Rollers is successful, then the winner will be the pastor with the fastest lap time. Are there any questions?"

"At least we won't be head to head with Dr. Stan," the Presbyterian minister muttered. "I'd rather take my chances with Satan."

"Men and women of God, please start your engines!"

The crowd roared while Roger and the other ministers walked to their newly customized cars.

"In the beginning was the Ford!" the anchorman shouted into his microphone.

Luther's Angel inched from the infield to the starting line. Angelina high-fived Satan through her Mustang's open window before the moped sputtered off to its sixty-six yard head start.

"Let the hindmost take the Devil!"

To the grandstand's delight, Angelina broke her tires loose in a cloud of red clay, then straightened her wheels and sped off. The track wasn't sharply banked, and her Mustang nearly spun out rounding the first turn. She caught the moped just before the final corner of the half-mile oval. But Satan kept a few feet in front of her pink bumper, weaving from side to side, so she couldn't pass. The moped entered the Eye of the Needle first, and the crowd groaned.

"The race is not always to the swift," the anchorman mournfully pronounced. "Or the battle to the strong."

Angelina drove back to the infield, got out of her car, and kneeled to the disappointed crowd. Women wept and applauded. Most of the men in the grandstand took off their NASCAR caps and held them over their hearts while the anchor from WFOP put his arm fraternally around her shoulder. "Where is Danica Patrick when we need her, Reverend?"

Angelina took off her helmet, then shook down her honey-brown hair. Back on her feet, she traded her headgear for the anchor's microphone. "I don't think Danica made it through divinity school." She smiled in the direction of *The Serpent Handler*. "At least not in my denomination."

The Presbyterian minister was up next, in *The Plymouth Rock*. He drove as if he were trying to avoid getting a speeding ticket in a hospital zone. He never got past second gear in his old steel gray column-shifter, and he didn't even manage to narrow the gap between himself and Satan before the moped triumphantly threaded itself through the Eye of the Needle. Roger couldn't help shaking his head when *The Plymouth Rock* stalled between the haystacks, sitting there like a deadbeat stuck at a toll booth. Several cameramen from the TV station finally pushed him through to the other side.

"God is gracious and merciful," the anchor declaimed.

"We want Bo!" somebody yelled from the top of the grandstand. "We want Bo Pritchard!" Bo had crashed his Camaro into a telephone pole ten years ago.

"And slow to anger!"

Psalm 145. Roger wondered whether the anchor from WFOP had cribbed a bunch of one-liners with the help of an internet concordance, or whether he actually read the Bible in his spare time.

§

THE CARS FROM Brushy Creek Bible, Connection Fellowship, Higher Calling Ministries, Trinity Anglican, Pentecostal Holiness, Carpenter's Tabernacle, Mount Carmel AME, and Church of the Redeemer all ended up pretty much like *Luther's Angel*. They spun their tires with spirit, they managed to catch Satan before the finish line, but they couldn't pass to get through the Eye of the Needle first.

Now only two Faster Pastors remained: Reverend Roger Rogers and Dr. Stan Dammers.

"Brothers and Sisters, I give you *The Serpent Handler*!"

"Good luck, Stan," Roger said through the open window of his Chevrolet.

"Luck has nothin' to do with it. Faith, hope, and horsepower. And the greatest of these—" Stan revved his engine until the crowd gave him a standing ovation. Once at the starting line, he never broke his tires loose or lost traction, and he maneuvered himself six inches behind the moped's taillight before they were halfway around the dirt track. Satan glanced back and gave him a gloved middle finger. From the Alianthus convertible, Stan Dammers returned the gesture, to the grandstand's delight.

The Alianthus drifted inside, then outside, then inside again, but the moped mirrored its every move as they went through the final corner.

The Eye of the Needle

Now the Alianthus accelerated into the moped's rear wheel and turned Satan fully sideways. *The Inferno* skidded into the stacked hay bales, raising a halo of loose straw, while Dr. Stan raced through the Eye of the Needle. On the far side, he bolted out of his car, tore off his helmet and shouted, "Get thee behind me, Satan!"

The crowd was cheering, wildly, stamping their feet, waving their caps at the simmering midsummer sun. Dr. Stan belted himself back into his Alianthus convertible for a victory lap.

But by then, Roger had already flung open the door of the *Jesus of Malibu* and had started sprinting toward the finish line. Satan was lying on the red clay, motionless, arms and legs akimbo, perhaps ten feet from *The Inferno*. The slender figure in Roger's arms seemed weightless as he carried it around the hay bales to the first aid station. But the only ones on duty were Hilda and her husband, Noel, with nothing but water bottles for dehydrated spectators.

"Oh my Lord," she said, covering her mouth with her left hand. "Is Satan OK?"

"Don't look at me," Noel insisted. "I'm calling 911."

Praying he wouldn't have to administer CPR, Roger gently removed Satan's helmet. Long, glossy hair fell to the ground like the petals from an enormous black pansy. The young woman seemed to be mumbling something in another language, then lost consciousness. Two thin trickles of mascara snaked past her perfect nose.

He heard Hilda say, "Didn't she used to do the weather?"

Satan opened her eyes just as Roger was getting ready to do his first compression. "*Perdóname!*" Somehow her ragged whisper was coming through the sound system, too. Her eyes seemed focused on something well beyond his face. She took his head in her hands, and she pressed her lips against his astonished mouth.

Wolf whistles and rebel yells crashed down from the grandstand like a tsunami. Now all Roger could see were cameras and Litepanels and WFOP logos.

"He shall bruise her head," the anchorman pronounced. "And she shall bruise his heel." He sounded relieved. "Ladies and gentlemen, it is finished. Please join me in congratulating *The Serpent Handler* on his well-earned victory. And have a safe drive home."

"I can't see any scriptural justification for this," Hilda said, wiping the corner of her eye with a wadded tissue. "But I'm happy for both of them."

"Hell yes." Noel pointed to the cameramen surrounding the first aid station, all of them facing the other way now, panning the grandstands for background footage. "This is gonna make the *network* news!"

"I never got to first base with Jésus before," Satan whispered, risen to her knees now, so close that Roger could feel her hot breath on his ear. "You can save me." He wondered whether it was only her concussion speaking, or whether he was hearing the gospel truth from her battered, beautiful heart. While they were waiting for the ambulance to arrive, he figured it couldn't hurt to borrow a Magic Marker and write his cellphone number on the side of her scarlet helmet.

Tails

YES, I DID ATTEMPT TO BOARD my ex-wife's Aegean kitten at Barkingham Palace. But there was absolutely no malice involved. The animal was legally transported, for its own physical safety. Like the Elgin marbles in 1816. Look it up on the internet if you don't believe me.

Susan called me out of the Caribbean blue on July 4. She and Dr. Bradley Young were celebrating what she called their "conjugal anniversary" on Barbados. I hadn't seen either of them in years. I'm here in this little shack up in the mountains, and they live down in a Belladonna "starter mansion" that probably set them back a couple million bucks. Where they're planning to finish, God only knows.

I'm not God, and I was more than a little pissed. I asked her how she got my cell number.

"From the Highway Department," she said. "Do you mind if I put you on speakerphone?"

I've been working for Greenville County DOT for going on thirty years. Now I'm the Pavement Inspector General. I don't call in the potholes and toss the dead animals into the back of a truck anymore. Now I'm a little further up the food chain. I got to make up my own title during the last fiscal year, in lieu of an annual increment. Hey, it helped balance the budget. You know what that's like. I drive a Crown Vic Police Interceptor that's been passed down from your motor pool, and I check every road repair request a week after I get the Completion Confirmation—to make sure it's been done right. And if it hasn't been done right, I send the asphalt truck out there again. For me, it's a matter of principle. *It's through the small things that we develop our moral imagination.* Alexander McCall Smith.

"I told them it was an emergency," she said. "And I might have mentioned my former name."

"That might be illegal," I said. "At the very least, it's unethical."

"I'm sorry, Doug," she said. "I didn't know what else I could do."

"Lead with your ovaries, Susan." I recognized Bradley's voice. Or perhaps I should call him Dr. Young. He used to be our Relationship Imperfection Coordinator, before he helped Susan discover her inner being—which eventually advised her to evict my outer being from what had been our household. "Stay on task," he whispered. "This isn't a nurturing situation."

So she told me they were two thousand miles away, on the Platinum Coast, at Dr. Phil's favorite resort. Dr. Phil is Bradley's role model. While they were getting ready to lock up their SM in Belladonna, they couldn't find their new kitten. For some unfathomable reason, it liked to hide ever since they'd bought it. They kept their limo driver waiting for a half hour while they opened every closet and looked under every piece of furniture in the goddamn place. "But we couldn't risk missing our flight. So we left Klitty a bowl full of Sheba and made sure her water station was working. And her Latrina."

I asked her about the etymology of her cat's name.

"It's short for Klytemnestra. That's with a *K*."

I asked her if she'd been taking spelling lessons from Bradley.

"Klitty's an Aegean. It's the only Greek breed in existence. Bradley and I felt like affirming her heritage."

My maternal grandmother was born in Macedonia, so I didn't feel like dignifying that remark with a response.

"She has to be hungry by now. Just drive over to our SM and bring her to Mew Gardens, on Woodruff Road. She has a reservation."

I reminded her she lived in a gated community. To keep out people like me.

"I've called Belladonna Security and given you a one-day pass code." She read me the ten-digit number, and I wrote it down. "You'll find the house key in a magnetic box under the rear bumper of Bradley's Hummer."

I told her I'd read somewhere that Belladonna had three-car garages.

"Bradley always leaves the Hummer in the driveway."

"It's too ballsy for the garage," he said. "It'd hit the ceiling."

"You'll find her cage on the kitchen counter," Susan continued. "And if you try using the code after today, you'll be arrested. Bradley insists that I set limits."

"Thank you, Bradley," I said.

"You're welcome, Doug," he said. "Within your twenty-four-hour window."

§

BUT KLITTY WAS NO longer welcome at Mew Gardens. When she didn't show up for her pre-boarding exam on Thursday, her bungalow had been given away to a deserving Siamese. I found this out when I called Mew Gardens for directions. It's easy to get lost on Woodruff Road, even if you've been living in Greenville County your whole life. Buildings and businesses appear and disappear like mushrooms, and nobody believes in numbering anything. "It's a holiday weekend," the business manager told me on the phone. "Every decent vet is slammed to the ceiling. There probably isn't an empty cat cage in the county."

"There's no place I can take her?"

I must have sounded desperate, because she put me on hold while she did some research. "Well, you might try Barkingham Palace," she said. "I recommend them highly. They're just across the street, and they're starting an affirmative action program for felines."

§

AFTER I'D VERIFIED the opening at Barkingham Palace, I brought Scenic out to the Crown Vic and put him in the back seat, behind the security screen. You can't leave a spider monkey alone for any longer than you'd leave a two-year-old. So I take him to work every day. He gets a real kick out of the blue lights and the siren.

We've been living together for years. A couple of months after Susan threw me out, I found him keening next to the flattened carcass of his mother on Highway 11. God knows how the both of them got there. After I used my Removall to shovel what was left of her into the back of my pickup truck, he tossed his tail over the trailer hitch and pulled himself right up on the rear bumper. I banged the Removall against the bedliner, but he wouldn't budge, and he wouldn't stop howling, so I finally gave him the banana from my lunch bucket. *And thereby hangs a tale.* William Shakespeare.

I decided to call him Scenic, because all the road signs up here say "Scenic Highway 11" and I felt like affirming his heritage. Scenic sounded better than my other options.

You can train a spider monkey to do almost anything. The litterbox was pretty tough, because they have to poop about every ten minutes, but he hasn't had an accident in years. Not even in the Crown Vic, which now has its own Monkey Loo. He goes down the driveway for the newspaper in the morning. He helps me empty the dishwasher, as long as I open the cabinets for him first. Hell, he'll even get me a beer while I'm watching TV. That's more than I could ever get Susan to do, and she used to be a waitress.

But I have to admit she gave me a valid security code. I bleeped my way into Belladonna on the first try, and only one house on Fairway Drive had a Hummer in plain sight. Its vanity plate read LOVE DR, so I knew I was in the right place. For a second I thought about giving it a good smack, but the damn thing was jacked up so high I could've busted my windshield. Not to mention turning their house key into collateral damage.

The house itself looked pretty stupid. Tuscan architecture doesn't really go with three-car garages. From the foyer I could see straight through to the kitchen, where Klitty was posing on the polished marble counter. She looked like a miniature Holstein—mostly white, with a little black saddle on her back. Her coat was maybe as long as Scenic's. Even though I could still smell a little Sheba in her dish, she didn't struggle when I put her inside the cage. Maybe she just wasn't hungry. Maybe she was relieved to see somebody other than Susan and Bradley. Maybe she could tell I detested LOVE DR.

I brought her out to my car, and I put her cage on the front seat. You could see her little pink nose through the skinny chrome bars on the top of it. Scenic was hanging on the Crown Vic's security screen, amusing himself by trying to stick his tail through the holes. He does things like that. When the kitten hissed and fanged him, he let out his loudest screech. "Mind your manners," I said. "You'll only have to put up with her for a couple of minutes."

§

THE RECEPTION AREA OF Barkingham Palace had Union Jack wallpaper, urine resistant laminate flooring, and only three chairs. When I came in with Klitty, the chairs were already taken—by a toy poodle with a rhinestone collar, a silver cocker spaniel in a polo pullover, and some muzzled monster in a pink tutu. Underneath the third dog was somebody in a matching T-shirt proclaiming PROUD PARTNER OF A TRANSGENDER PIT BULL.

I walked up to the receptionist and told her I was bringing a kitten to be boarded for the week. I mentioned that I'd already called and been pre-approved on the affirmative action program. She looked up from her Yphone and said, "Are you the responsible party?"

"Yes," I said. "In a sense."

"Then I'll need your credit card information."

I told her I left my credit card at home, but she could get the number by calling Mew Gardens. "That's where she's usually taken, but they're full."

Note my meticulous use of the passive voice.

"What's the animal's name?"

"Klytemnestra," I said, and then I spelled it for her.

"It should be in our database. We're owned by the same British conglomerate." She did something with her Yphone that I couldn't even begin to explain. "Here it is, Dr. Young. We've already got your signature on file." She pointed to the digital billboard reading PLEASE STAND IF ABLE in a running red headline. "I hope you don't mind. I think your pet's lighter than everybody else's."

The old lady with the poodle said, "I'm allergic to cats."

"So is Ralph Lauren," the young woman said, tugging on the drawstring of his polo pullover. She looked like a refugee from a runway—all legs and lips and eyeliner, and almost as skinny as Susan the day I married her. She took a dust mask out of her purse and draped it over her dog's nostrils. "I hope he doesn't go into anaphylactic shock."

"You can thtand over here." The Proud Partner talked like Tweetie Bird in the old cartoons, but without the attitude. I was informed that Ashley didn't pay any attention to cats.

Between the T-shirt and the tutu, I figured Ashley was—or had been—a he. "If you don't mind my asking," I said, "how did you discover your dog's . . . tendencies?"

"When Samantha moved out on me, she left six of her dresses in the closet. I was so sad I couldn't throw them out. As soon as I got the puppy, he started to sleep on them. Then he started to sleep *inside* them. I thought he was sending me a message."

I told the Proud Partner it made perfectly good sense to me.

"And on play dates, he'd only sniff the unneutered males. Subsequently he started to—display. That's when I sewed him some dresses of her own."

The old lady with the poodle clutched it more tightly to her midriff bulge.

"That's pretty pervy," the receptionist said.

For a minute nobody else said anything.

The young woman with Ralph Lauren finally muttered, "Awent you afwaid thomebody will get tied to the back of a twuck?"

"Please stop threatening her," the Proud Partner said.

"I'm not thweatening *her*."

I sidestepped over to the plate glass door with the royal family stenciled on it, and I pushed it open with the bottom corner of Klitty's cage. The cat began yowling. "I'm sorry," I said, nodding my head toward the digital billboard. "She can't stand it."

§

I TRIED KEEPING Klitty at my place for the rest of the day. It wasn't a good idea. The first thing she did when I opened her cage was to squat in Scenic's Monkey Loo. He let out his loudest screech, and he yanked her out by the tail. When she peed in his face, he screeched again before he dumped the whole box of cedar shavings on the floor.

So I put Klitty back in her carrier, in protective custody, while I tried to calm Scenic down. "She'll have her own box," I promised. "I'll put it in the other room." But Scenic was bouncing off walls like an oversized racquetball with a prehensile tail. I thought he'd forgiven me after I fed him his favorite tropical fruit compote for dinner. But he barfed while we were watching beach volleyball on ESPN.

After I changed my shirt, I checked my watch. My one-day pass code would be good until midnight, and it was only 9:45 p.m. I had ten days of paid vacation coming. Maybe this would work out better in Belladonna.

§

AT FIRST IT WORKED out better than I'd hoped. On the way over, I stopped off at the Econoclast in Belladonna Commons, right outside the security gate, where they had specials on Bud Light, ripple chips, microwavable soups, and bananas—enough to take care of me and Scenic for the week. I wasn't about to raid Bradley's refrigerator. *Eat not to dullness.* Benjamin Franklin.

Klitty had plenty of Sheba in the pantry.

I also brought in the portable Monkey Loo from the back seat of the Crown Vic. I set it up in the great room, on the opposite side of the plasma TV from Klitty's Latrina. I didn't want the whole week turning into a pissing contest, even if it wasn't in my house.

Say what you want about Bradley—he's got a great cable package. I'd be able to watch all of the Manchester United friendlies while they were on their Southeast Asia tour—Bangkok, Sidney, Yokohama. The only thing was, the network had some idiot doing the play-by-play who'd probably missed the cut for their American sports broadcasts. He kept calling the player in front of the net a "goaltender," like he was talking about a hockey game.

"Look at that goaltender punt! He could play in the NFL!"

"He's a goal*keeper*, asshole!" I get excited when I'm watching TV sports on a really big screen. "And longer isn't better in European football. It just gives the defenders a chance to get under the damn thing."

Scenic started jumping up and down on the other Stressless lounge chair, in complete agreement.

Now the idiot was giving last week's score lines with Manchester United first, even though they weren't the home team. I tried muting the sound, but whenever I did it, the set automatically switched to Closed Caption, which was even worse. I finally just turned down the volume as low as it'd go, and I chomped on some ripple chips whenever the guy started talking.

After the first goal, Scenic hopped down to the floor and started kicking one of Klitty's toys towards her open cage, which doubled as her day bed. I had to admit it was kind of shaped like a soccer goal, even if it didn't have a net. Klitty was awake, so she batted the thing back to him with her front paw. They kept it up for nearly half an hour, until the doorbell rang.

"Play on," I told them. "I'll get it."

§

It was Belladonna Security. While he was doing his sunset drive-by, Sergeant Sandy Blessington had seen my Crown Vic parked next to the Hummer. He knew the Youngs were out of town for the week.

I told him I was Susan's ex-husband, and I explained the cat-sitting snafu. You old enough to know what that word really means?

"Sorry," he said, handing back my Pavement Inspector General ID card. "Just doing my job."

Then I invited him inside for a beer.

"What the hell," he said. He took off his glasses and rubbed his eyes. "I'll be retiring in three weeks."

I knew I recognized him, but I couldn't remember from where, and I'd never set foot in Belladonna before. "Me neither," he grinned at me. "Not when I was a real cop."

I asked him if he'd ever worked the northern end of the county.

"Couple of years. Just before I finished my twenty."

"I think I saw you up over by Doc Graves's place. Right after he died."

"Yeah. He was a good one, God rest his soul. Gave me my first pair of glasses when I was just a kid. Went out of his way to help people. Not like the pricks who live in these new places." He swigged his latest beer, then waved the empty bottle. "She's got considerable nerve, asking you to take care of her cat."

"What I don't understand," I said, "is why she didn't ask you."

You know Sandy Blessington. Everything about him's big, including his laugh. "Belladonna Security doesn't do pets." The kitten had jumped into his lap, and she was snuggling against his holster. "It's in the covenant. We have to draw the line somewhere."

"I hear you," I said. Scenic handed me a bag of ripple chips, then waited for me to open it up and give him one. "I hear you."

"That is one hell of a monkey," Sandy Blessington said.

§

FOR THE REST OF the week, Sandy stopped by on his rounds every night. We'd sit in the dual Stressless loungers, Klitty on his lap, Scenic on mine. It turned out Sandy was a big fan of Mixed Martial Arts. I'd watched it once in a while, when there was nothing else on, but I didn't know jack. To me, it just looked like a couple of Navy Seals who'd had way too many brewskies trying to kill each other. He patiently explained the different fighting styles—clinch maulers, bangers, pound and ground, sprawl and brawl.

"It's not mortal combat," Sandy said. "Did you know there's less major injuries in MMA than boxing or football? And it's not even close."

"Jesus," I said. They were introducing the fighters for the next bout. "Just look at the muscles on that little guy."

"Now you're sounding like a real nut hugger," Sandy sniggered. "All of the featherweights are really ripped. Pound for pound, they're probably the best athletes on the planet."

Sandy was off on Saturdays, but he stopped by anyway to watch the MMA Super Heavyweight title fight on a ninety-inch screen. Did you see it? We were both rooting for the underdog, because the champ kept trash talking like a real turd. When our guy got him in an Achilles lock, I high-fived Sandy and gave Scenic a little sip of my Bud Light.

§

"This is why I divorced him," Susan said.

She and Bradley were standing right there in the foyer, with their matching Louis Vuittons. I'd forgotten they'd already spent a day in Barbados before they'd called me. I was thinking they wouldn't be back in Belladonna till tomorrow.

"And you," she said, pointing at Sandy. "Put down my Klitty, or I'll call the police."

"Ma'am, I am the police." Sandy wasn't in uniform, so he took out his wallet and showed her his gold shield. Now he stroked Klitty with his free hand. "Your animal is perfectly safe. I'm just here checking up on her."

"Have a Bud Light," I said to Bradley. "They're all mine. I promise."

He ignored me and turned to his significant outer being. That's his term, not mine. "Let the world know how you feel, Susan. Embrace yourself as a fully actualized person."

She gave her own breasts the obligatory hug, which I remembered all too well from our last counseling session. "I'm trying, Bradley."

"Remember what I taught you, Susan. Otherwise men like Doug will be telling you what to do for the rest of your life. Visualize the video."

The fight was over, so I figured I might as well turn off the TV.

"Bradley's just filmed an instructional DVD. *Gender Assertiveness for MDs*. Our neighbor is the executive producer for the series, and he commissioned it. Ted Dickey. He lives down the street."

I generally don't watch anything in the self-help genre, but I'll admit I've taken a peek at *Civil Service for Mental Defectives*. I wondered if Bradley and Susan knew the MD logo isn't a doctor, but a monkey with a mortarboard. He even looks a little bit like Scenic. But all I said was, "That's very nice." I wasn't confrontational.

"Bradley's a PhD," Susan said, to no one in particular. "*And* a certified tai chi instructor."

That really ticked me off. I dropped out of college because I didn't want to trust my education to ex-hippies who never read books and who spent most of their time on exercise mats. And don't even get me started on graduate assistants. The last time I spoke with one was in a bar in Simpsonville ten years ago. ABD in sociology. She thought William James was Jesse's brother. When I told her I was an autodidact, she asked me if I could teach her father how to fix her Toyota. Swear to God.

Now Susan looked at Sandy while she pointed to Bradley. "He'll be contacting your supervisor."

When Sandy put Klitty on the floor, you could see the belt with his service revolver. And when he stood up, he was tall as Bradley—maybe six-six—and about twice as wide. "That's nice to know, ma'am. But my retirement paperwork's already been processed."

"Don't shoot!" Bradley shouted. Then he started blubbering something about being self-insured.

Scenic screeched and ran into the powder room. He doesn't like loud noises, especially when they're being made by a guy who looks like John Tesh. "Relax," I said to Susan. "He always puts the seat back down." I followed him in and flushed—twice, I admit, for the dramatic effect. Then I took Scenic and the Monkey Loo out to the Crown Vic, and we drove home. You don't need a security code to get *out* of Belladonna.

That's when Susan decided to get Gender Assertive. And when she decided to call you. The real police. You know Sandy, right? He'll back me up on everything I've said. One hundred percent. Hell, we were just watching TV. *Reality leaves a lot to the imagination.* John Lennon. You've heard of him? I'm impressed. He's been dead for a pretty long time.

Confessions

THE CHRISTMAS EVE SERVICE at Belladonna Methodist Church would begin at sundown, so even the toddlers wouldn't snore into their Snuggies. It was just one of the many user-friendly reforms that Reverend Roger Rogers had devised since he'd descended upon upstate South Carolina three years ago.

Half an hour early, Hilda Willis had spirited in her husband, Noel, by the elbow of his Clemson windbreaker. They were sitting, front and center, in the first pew, within sneezing distance of the communion rail. Noel's mucous membranes always acted up in December. She hoped the reverend had remembered to install the hypoallergenic altar candles she'd donated the week before—when Noel had finally promised to attend this special service. She hadn't been able to find fragrance-free personal candles for the entire congregation. But those hand-held minis would be burning only during the final carol, when a little sniffling would be more than appropriate.

Although they couldn't see the congregation behind them, the white noise of holiday good wishes was filling their ears. Ever since the new preacher had come from California with a surfboard perched on top of his Chevy Malibu like a giant ichthys, empty pews at Belladonna Methodist had been hard to find. Noel wedged his so-called personal candle into the hymnal rack and glanced down at the three-color program entitled *Rambling with ROAR*. "Who's ROAR?"

"Roger Olmstead Audubon Rogers," Hilda whispered back. "His parents are prominent environmentalists."

"You said they were hippies."

"Well, they matured before they decided to have children." Hilda smiled at her spouse, who often referred to himself as Saint Darwin of Galapagos. "Organisms do change over time. Bless their hearts."

The reverend strode up to the altar from behind the giant Chrismon tree, which was covered with Latin, Celtic, Jerusalem, Eastern, anchor, triumphal, and even Upsilon crosses. Lambs and lions dangled among them, and a glowing nativity star nearly scraped the sanctuary's vaulted ceiling. In honor of the occasion, the reverend was wearing his white vestments, instead of his usual basic black. Because he'd given the choir and the church pianist the evening off, no ear-catching coda announced his arrival—so he tapped the lapel microphone on his organic cotton alb. Then he began reciting Luke's version of the first Christmas.

After the gospel had returned the shepherds to their field and to their flock, proclaiming the Good News to any mammal who'd listen, Reverend Rogers asked for some help in singing "Away in a Manger," even though it wasn't on the program. By the fifth note, Hilda's lead soprano had fully superseded the reverend's reedy tenor, and he gladly turned off his microphone for the duration.

But the music was no mere serendipity. In seminary, Reverend Rogers had been informed by his Pastoral SWOTs Assessment that his greatest strength was "sincerely organized spontaneity." So he'd determined the casual segue to his Christmas Eve sermon months before. He told his congregation that yes, Jesus had spent His very first night in a manger, that He had no crib for His bed, and that He indeed had reclined on the hay. But the rest of James R. Murray's hymn was not entirely accurate. "The little Lord Jesus did make a cry—in fact, He made lots of them—as any composer who'd ever given birth would certainly know." He waited for the maternal giggles to subside before he continued. "Yes, the stars might have been shining in the sky, but I doubt whether they could have looked straight down though the stable roof." The men joined in, with their deeper laughter. "And what about that 'sweet head'? It must have been sniffing a lot of animal poop." Now he had the teenagers' snickering attention. "Mary and Joseph had loving hearts, all right, but they didn't have Luvs—or Pampers—so the Savior's own first gift to the world must have added to that humble bouquet."

Noel sneered audibly behind *Rambling with ROAR*.

"And those shepherds who saw the angel in the field, and then journeyed to see Him in His helplessness, probably didn't smell too good, either." Reverend Rogers spread the voluminous sleeves of his vestments before he inhaled, beaming at Hilda. "Certainly nothing like these magnificent candles."

Hilda blushed deeply, snatching Noel's program and scribbling on it with her pew pencil. POETIC LICENSE. FRAGRANCE FREE.

Now Reverend Rogers settled himself in front of the communion rail. Dozens of tiny sneakers, most of them lighting up like hazard flashers, thudded down the carpeted aisle. All the girls kneeled to the right of Hilda, and all the boys lowered their rumps to the left of Noel, who prudently retracted his feet as far as his arthritic knees would permit. The reverend swung his gaze from one side to the other, smiling upon every child before he spoke a single word. "Who can remember what day it is?"

They all could remember, in unison.

"That's right." He removed the advent crèche from the altar table and pointed to the empty manger. "And does anybody know who belongs in here?"

"JESUS!"

"And does anybody have any idea where Jesus is?" The reverend squinted up at the ceiling, shading his eyes with his hand.

The biggest boy took out a figurine half-swaddled in Kleenex from his own pocket, and he stifled a well-rehearsed sneeze.

Now the reverend lowered his gaze. "Bless you! Jesus is right here, right here among us. Let's put Him where he belongs on Christmas Eve." He extended the crèche, and the boy placed the miniature newborn inside the manger. The reverend tucked Him in securely, then returned the crèche to the altar table, between the two tallest candles. "And what sound does Jesus make?"

"BAAAAAA!" The tiniest girls had been practicing their bleats in Sunday School ever since the Chrismon tree went up. "'Cause He's the Lamb of God!"

The reverend turned to the boys. "And what other sound does Jesus make?"

"ARRRRRR! 'Cause He's a tiger!"

"No, he's a panther," the boy in the bright teal jacket said.

The reverend was delighted that all God's children were still remembering their lines. "And why's that?"

"Because the Bengals are gonna lose to San Diego. But the Panthers are gonna win!"

Now the whole congregation broke into whistles and cheers.

"Why isn't he a lion?" It was the toddler whose family had just moved to Belladonna from Kalamazoo, Michigan.

The biggest boy elbowed his new neighbor's ribs. "They can't even beat Buffalo!"

Reverend Rogers forced himself to laugh along with his congregation. But he'd scripted a few moments of comic relief, not an entire *SNL* skit. Now he'd *really* have to improvise. He lowered his head to toddler level and held his index finger in front of his lips. "God can take different forms for different people," he said, enunciating each word distinctly. "That's something our whole team needs to remember."

After the children had scampered back to their pews and their parents, Reverend Rogers led the group confession. "Almighty and merciful God, we have erred and strayed from Thy ways like lost sheep."

Baaa, humbug, Noel thought.

"We have followed too much the devices and desires of our own heart." Reverend Rogers felt his own voice tremble, and his own face fill with blood. "We have offended against Thy holy laws."

Standing at the back of the sanctuary, behind the very last pew, a study in black thought *Gracias a Dios*.

"We have left undone those things which we ought to have done, and we have done those things which we ought not to have done."

Yes, Hilda Willis thought, *but please tell me the difference. I need some help down here*.

"O God, have mercy upon us. Spare those who confess their faults to Thee." Reverend Rogers always allotted thirty seconds for silent prayer, which he discreetly monitored with his digital sports watch. "Amen."

Now the reverend announced—for the benefit of visitors—that tonight's communion was entirely open. Not just for members of the church, but for anyone who welcomed the spirit of God in this special season. He put on his serving gloves before he lifted the loaf of artisan bread from the salver beside the chalice. "We'll dip our own," he said. "Proceeding from the front."

Hilda grabbed Noel by the elbow again, and he didn't resist. He'd welcome God whenever—even if the Holy Spirit wouldn't be ringing his doorbell anytime soon. At least he didn't have a wheat allergy. After he'd bloodied his bread with Welch's and popped it into his mouth, Noel dropped a check payable to the Pastor's Emergency Fund onto the empty salver. This year, he'd be subsidizing the electric bills of the unemployed, so Duke Energy wouldn't have to raise his rates to cover the shortfall. It was a shell game. Noel was pretty sure they couldn't legally turn off anyone's power during the winter months.

Hilda patted his empty hand before they returned to their seats to watch the rest of the congregation be served. Martha Brown came up in her portable wheelchair, pushed by her husband, Clayton. She held her little dog in her lap, hind legs tucked under the hem of her sweater. Elise and Gary Michel, still rosy from their afternoon ride, hadn't changed out of their reflective cycling suits. They looked shiny as a couple of Christmas presents. The Sorensens wore hand-painted scarves—Jorja's latest creations, no doubt—knotted above the collars of their all-weather coats. Harold and Lois Carmichael walked down the aisle in a tuxedo and an evening gown, respectively—probably on their way to some fundraiser at Bullpen College, where Harold was Vice President for Athletic Development. The slow-motion parade of holiday hoodies, hiking boots, and reindeer neckties lasted for nearly three Ytune arrangements of "I'll Be Home for Christmas." The last communicant wore a lace mantilla shrouding her face and shoulders, and she dropped to her knees in front of the minister. He smiled before breaking the last sliver of bread in half. She dipped hers into the chalice first, and she raised the crust to her mouth, without raising her head, before he'd finished immersing his own.

Mid-note, the music stopped. The reverend started walking down the center aisle, using an altar candle to light the stubby ones closest to him, on either side. Then the flickering was passed down every pew—lit candle vertical, unlit horizontal—toward the stained glass windows that now held only darkness behind them. Somebody turned off the recessed lights in the ceiling, and in the candles' gathering glow they sang the first verse of "Silent Night." While the congregation left the sanctuary, family by family, row by row, Hilda went to the communion rail for an extra holiday prayer. When she closed her eyes, she could smell the Chrismon tree for the first time. *Noël to the spirit of Noel, Noël to the spirit of Noel, Noël to the spirit of Noel* . . . .

"I think somebody's waiting for us, Hilda. He probably hasn't had his supper yet."

She rose slowly from her knees and joined her husband. In the empty narthex, she thanked the reverend for his service.

"Please—call me Roger." As usual, he raised his eyebrows to give his elderly congregants a better view of his blue eyes. "Or ROAR, if you prefer."

Then Hilda knew that her prayers were about to be answered, if she just gave them a little help. "Oh, dear. I think I need to visit the rest room. Noel, could you keep Roger company until I come back?"

Noel had just dropped his annotated *Rambling with ROAR* into the recycling bin. "Certainly."

After Hilda was out of earshot, Roger said, "I see you're a Clemson fan."

Noel fingered the white paw on the side pocket of his orange jacket. "I'm not really a fan. I went to school there." Now he pointed to the reverend's elaborately embroidered vestments. "Jesus ever wear one of those?"

"It's a little over the top. I only bring it out for special occasions. My parents bought it for me when I graduated seminary."

Noel asked if they'd had to mortgage the commune.

"Organic farm," Roger said. "They've done pretty well for themselves."

Greenwashers. "I'll bet."

"So what did you think of my sermon?" Roger knew Hilda's husband was a retired biology teacher. "Scientifically accurate?"

Noel closed his eyes for a moment and nodded in silence.

"Glad to hear it. From our very own Carl Sagan."

Noel couldn't stop himself now. "So let me get this straight, ROAR. You believe in a god who can summon angels and raise people from the dead, but who can't come up with a pacifier and an air freshener?"

Roger ran his fingers through his curly blond hair and felt the corners of his mouth turning upwards. He enjoyed a spiritual challenge. "Just let me put the chalice away, Noel, and then we can talk theology."

"Thanks but no thanks," Noel muttered, examining the oatmeal-colored walls for something of at least minimal intellectual interest. He walked from bulletin board to bulletin board, filled with recipes and holiday makeover hints and crayon angels and Termite Basketball schedules. Then he started counting the used candles in the wicker basket next to the door.

When Hilda came back from the bathroom, she wasn't alone. "Look who's thinking of joining our congregation, Noel!" The final communicant stood beside her.

"It's not *our*—"

The woman removed her black shawl, baring her braided hair and her bosomy sweater.

"My husband and I always watched you on WFOP, Teresa. It used to be the high point of our evenings."

Noel managed to mumble something about the Dark Corner Speedway before his wife gently stepped on his shoe.

"Oh yes," Teresa said. "When Roger saved me, after my accident."

Teresa Torrido—nicknamed The Weather Tootsie by Hilda and Noel—had crashed her moped during an interfaith fundraiser, and the reverend had carried her from the dirt track before the ambulance arrived.

"We were there," Hilda said. "Volunteering at the first aid station. But you wouldn't remember us."

"Oh yes," Teresa said. "And Roger is so kind. And so I am here."

"Amen to that," Noel said, trying his level best to keep his eyes focused upon only The Weather Tootsie's face. "You were going along pretty good until that guy in the Alianthus took you out. I don't think the reverend could've caught you."

Her teeth were dazzling even in the near dark. "I am so much faster than he is."

Hilda started coughing, pointing toward the candles.

"I thought they were fragrance-free," Noel said.

"Just the votives. Not the personals." When Hilda managed to catch her breath again, she turned back to Teresa and asked what she'd been doing since she left WFOP.

"Special events. Like the race. And corporate retreats. Team building. Intimacy seminars." She licked her glossy lips. "They pay so much better than the TV station."

Now Roger emerged from the sanctuary. He was wearing a rumpled gray blazer over a white T-shirt. In his street clothes he looked, Hilda thought, like a Hollywood celebrity trying his best not to be recognized in public.

"*Gracias a Dios*," Teresa said, striding towards him.

When he repeated her words and put his right arm around her sweater, she leaned her cheekbone into his shoulder. "Teresa will be joining our congregation very soon," he smiled. "It's still our little secret."

§

I DIDN'T SAY ANYTHING to Hilda while we walked out to the parking lot. I didn't want to interrupt whatever hymn she was humming to the entire cosmos. And when she sat down inside the car I didn't tell her the hem of her coat was hanging out over the rocker panel. I just flipped it onto the floor mat before I closed the door.

On the drive back to our condo, she opened her mouth just long enough to thank me for coming to church with her. "You don't know how important it is to me, Noel."

Then she started humming again.

I told her I knew, and that was why I went.

Now somebody was sniffling, and it wasn't me. The Belladonna holiday traffic was pretty heavy, but I tried sneaking a peek at Hilda's face. The instrument lights weren't bright enough to let me see anything. "I thought I was the one with the allergies," I said, refocusing on the road so I wouldn't collide with a power pole decorated like a giant candy cane.

Hilda doesn't talk that much, but when she gets started sometimes she just can't stop. Turns out she'd gotten the church candles at the Econoclast for half price—with an extra five percent off for her senior discount. She gave me chapter and verse for every sermon Reverend ROAR had preached during the month of December. A new baby was baptized last Sunday, and after the service she went up to congratulate the parents. They told her how much they'd enjoyed hearing her in the choir. "The man asked if I'd ever sung professionally. And when the wife saw my wedding ring, she wanted to know when my husband had died."

"What did you tell her?"

"I said you were sick."

"Really?"

"You were so good at the church tonight, Noel. Fellowshipping with Roger. And with Teresa, too."

I could almost hear her smiling. "Let's invite The Weather Tootsie over to our place sometime," I said. "Along with her new boyfriend."

Her fingers began playing with the sleeve of my jacket. "They do make the cutest couple, don't you think? He's even prettier than she is."

"Yes," I admitted. "But it's damn close."

"And he's so good with children. Bless his heart. I hope she is."

"She can baptize my inner baby anytime," I said. "With either font."

Hilda laughed out loud, something I wish she'd do more often. Then she thanked me for not saying anything about my inner baby in front of her minister.

"You're welcome," I said, as I pulled into the driveway and pressed the automatic opener for our garage.

While we were both watching the door shudder upwards, she said, "What did you and Roger talk about while I was in the bathroom with Teresa?"

And then I told her.

§

I DIDN'T SAY ONE blessed word to my husband until I'd microwaved his supper and gotten my own keys off the ring underneath the wall telephone. Noel had turned on the TV and was talking back to the screen. George Bailey was ready to jump off the bridge, but the Angel Second Class jumped in first, so George had to dive in to save him because Clarence didn't have his wings yet. "Give him a flotation device as a down payment!"

He was still laughing at his own joke when I said I had some last-minute shopping to do. I was already inside the garage, adjusting the front seat to Driver Number Two, before he could find the remote and hit the mute button and yell *Watch the crazies, Hilda, It's Christmas Eve!* through the wall.

I'd told him the truth, since I knew Meredith Cotten was having an open house for viewing the Universal Holiday Tree at Ecumenical Bedding. It was where we'd bought our new mattress, and I'd been back there for complimentary tea and nibbles with some of the other Methodist women. I could say I was looking for a new set of pillowcases. Since they're a nonprofit agency, they work out of their house, which is on the far end of Belladonna from our condo.

Meredith and her husband met me in the foyer, which has a ceiling almost as high as the one in our sanctuary. "You've caught us at a good time," she said. "Between the Primitive Baptists and the Episcopalians." I told them their tree looked like it belonged in a national park.

"Time to enhance the eggnog," Jimmy said. He asked me if I wanted some before he poured in the bourbon. Bless his heart.

"It's been a pretty slow night," Meredith said. She was wearing a red velvet Mrs. Claus evening gown. "So far."

"Virgin for Hilda," Jimmy said, handing me a brimming cup. "And for my very own special lady—"

When the doorbell rang out the first bars of "Santa Baby," she grabbed the second cup and told her husband to go make himself useful. Meredith grinned in my direction. "We've still got a few hours before the chimney closes."

At least a dozen couples, dressed to the nines, were coming through the front door. I asked Meredith if I could speak with her privately, as a friend, and she suggested we go upstairs. "We're the

Episcopalian pre-party. Before their midnight mass. We have the test mattresses down here, if anyone gets too fond of the egg nog."

Meredith walked me up the massive mahogany staircase. I'd never been on the second floor of her home, and I felt like I was on a private tour of the White House. She keyed open the deadbolt and led me inside an enormous room with a king-sized bed at its center. "Behold the *master* suite." Meredith winked. "But we women know *that's* a misnomer."

I explained how my husband had insulted my minister. How he'd gloated to me about it. How he was making fun of my favorite movie at this very moment. "I had to leave the house," I said. "I didn't trust myself to speak."

Meredith removed her holiday hat and placed it over the footboard. "I understand completely."

I asked her, as a woman of faith, for her advice.

Meredith vanished into her walk-in closet while my eyes adjusted to the mood lighting. I shouted, "I love your furniture!"

"They're my grandmother's antiques!" she shouted back. "That dresser belonged to Abigail Adams!"

When she came out, a silver necklace with dual pendants dangled between her breasts. "If Jimmy's misbehaving, I always wear this."

It looked a bit lopsided to me, but I said, "It's lovely."

"And when he *really* misbehaves . . ." She grasped the pendants and pulled, snapping the thin chain. "The breakaway clasp has a lifetime guarantee. Unlike most husbands." Then she handed the necklace to me. "My go-to holiday gift. Just tell Jimmy I'm waiting for him up here."

I went downstairs, holding my would-be Christmas present in my coat pocket. Jimmy was walking around with a pitcher of enhanced egg nog, telling everybody he was a High Anglican at heart. Two women cornered him and started complaining about their lower backs, wondering whether he or Meredith would be the best source for mattress advice.

I told them Meredith had gone upstairs for the evening.

"Talk to me ladies," Jimmy grinned. "Talk to me."

And when nobody was looking, I went to the far side of the tree and decorated the first empty branch I could find—between an

Episcopal Chick ornament and a sepia Jesus with a crown of thorns. It almost looked like it belonged there. Maybe if they'd been drinking enough egg nog those High Churchers would mistake it for enhanced tinsel.

§

DEAR GOD, ALMIGHTY CREATOR, Hilda Willis is a high-maintenance Christian. Forgive me for being angry when her cellphone interrupted You. I had to listen to her confession—or rather, her confession on behalf of her husband—and let her know I wasn't mad at Noel. I told her I can take a joke, and so can You. I told her Noel had a point, the whole ROAR business was silly—but it fills up the pews, and then we can go on from there. We can't just take the ones who already walk on water.

I hope I made her feel better. But Lord, that woman has been beating herself up in Your name for so many years that I probably made things worse.

When she thanked me for hearing her confession, I told her Methodist ministers don't do individual confessions. We do group confessions and spiritual counseling. We believe in the adequacy of the congregant before You.

Big mistake. So I shook my head at my Yphone and assured her it was a distinction without a difference, and she could think of it as a confession if she wanted to. But she probably shouldn't call me again until after she'd sat down and talked with her husband.

But I know how she feels. She wants to be deserving of You, and she doesn't understand how the person she loves could deny You.

Teresa. Dear Teresa.

After she'd crashed during that ridiculous Faster Pastor Challenge—the one I tried so hard to lie my way out of—I visited her at the hospital. The race was a farce but her injuries were real. She had a concussion and two broken ribs from that idiot Baptist who calls himself a high-performance vehicle of God. He just wanted to get his car through the Eye of the Needle first.

She told me the TV station's plan was to let me win, and all the other pastors had signed off on it. Stan Dammers was driving off script—but of course, You already know that. In the hospital, while she was still half woozy from the Percocet, she began telling me what a terrible woman she was. That she had broken every law of God and man. That she did not deserve to live. When I said she must be exaggerating, she took out her Yphone and showed me the pictures.

Why was I so happy to see them?

When I said Your mercy was infinite, and You had forgiven much worse, I saw in Teresa the beauty You see in all of us, even as we sin. I felt I had truly become Your love for the first time.

And when she told me, a week later, that she'd been dragged to Holy Communion for seventeen years, hating every minute of it, that she'd never been back since, and that she'd never touched You until she met me—well, that filled me with the sin against the Holy Ghost.

Lord, I love her because she believes she is evil, and because she believes only I have the power to change her.

She has already changed me—spirit, flesh, flesh, spirit, one and the same. And she has drawn me closer to Your love and farther away from You. And in my heart, I know—and I know You know—I would have it no other way. Spare those who confess their faults to Thee.

§

Perdóname Padre pues he pecado. You want me in English? Forgive me, Father, for I have sinned. Tonight I am here because I am a *borracha.* Full of the wine I was supposed to be saving for my wedding day. It is *once años*—*perdóname,* eleven years—since my last confession. Just the names of the husbands and the wives I have ruined would keep us here past the hour of the Savior's birth, and you would not believe me anyway. *Bueno.* So I will confine myself to only today.

Today I took the Methodist communion, and I took it with an impure heart. I took it from the minister who is the most beautiful man I have ever seen, in every way a man can be beautiful. If you saw him, you would agree with me. You would forsake your own vows. You would fall in love with him yourself. But all men are stupid, and the most beautiful ones, *gracias a Dios,* are the most stupid of all.

I lie to him by telling the truth. *Tanto mejor*. I say all the things I have done, all the things I am not telling you, and I show him the pictures to prove it. The ones of the husbands I have sent to the wives. The ones of the wives I have sent to the husbands. The ones I have sent to the little *niños*. My phone is the eye of God. And still he refuses to believe me. Would you like me to show you? Which ones? You will not say? Then you will have them all. You do not have to look. But you will know they are all on this little screen. You will see them in the eye of your mind, in the eye of your heart. *Listo? Uno. Dos. Tres.* Now here is the sound, just for you. He grunts like a *cochino*! Let him who has ears to hear, hear. Is that not what God Himself has said? Yes, He is a man, and so He is stupid, too.

But when I am with the man who will soon be my husband, married in his own church, I am not what I am. *Soy la nueva mujer.* I see in his blue eyes everything he believes me to be, despite what I have told him. Do you believe what he tells me? Do you believe I am a blessed creature of God? You do? Of course you do. Lie as you please.

You save your *cojones* for the little boys, not for me.

Now I will leave you to your God and to your Christmas. Another stupid man is waiting for me who is worth ten of you. A hundred. *Un millón.* And I will show him tonight the picture he has never seen before. The picture of the one we have made together. The picture of the one who will be worth more than God Himself, and the both of them will love me forever, until my soul is pure *corazón. Corazon*! Until it is the blessed heart of the little boy that is beating inside me.

Gato

TOMASA DIDN'T LIKE THE CAT, but Señora Carmichael thought it could do no wrong. By her order, it had the run of the entire house. No sooner would Tomasa vacuum one room than Whitsie would prance back inside, roll around with the catnip *ratón*—the brown of Tomasa's own skin—and leave a scattering of long white hair on the carpet, the deep blue of the ocean at Champerico. And, while she sighed mightily and vacuumed the floor again, it would move on to the next bedroom, and do the same thing. It was like trying to clean foam off the sea.

If she locked the cat in the Señora's walk-in closet, it would scratch furiously at the threshold, and Tomasa would have to free it before it tore the *preciado* carpet from the wooden strip beneath the door. On some days Tomasa would clean the house three times before the cat finally gave up and slept in its favorite spot of afternoon sun in the guest suite. This would happen just before Señora Carmichael came back from her shopping or from her church or from her exercise class at the college where her husband raised money.

Tomasa made certain the *gato* was really asleep—the Señora called it a Persian, but it never purred—before scurrying to scrub the bathrooms and the kitchen in half the time the Señora had said the job would take. And if she left the carpets for last, Whitsie would make them look like Tomasa had never touched them—like she had been watching *telenovelas* during the whole time she was supposed to be working. She told herself she was lucky to have the job, but she felt the way she did more than twenty years ago, in Guatemala, when she would go out in the fields with her new husband and the *criollo* would pay only for his work, not for hers. As if her work meant nothing. As if her work had not been done.

§

WHEN TOMASA WAS pregnant with Rafael—bless his soul!—she and her husband decided to leave the *finca* and come to California. Their son was born in America, in a clinic with a real doctor—not some *bruja* who didn't know what she was doing. And he was baptized by a real priest, not the *cofradía* who had married her to Jorge. Soon they moved to Greenville, South Carolina, because they wanted a place where it was not too cold and where it was not too close to the border or to the sea. A place where they wouldn't be asked for the papers they didn't have. A place where their son—and the two sons that soon followed—could go to school and learn to become *Americanos*.

For years, the five of them lived in a beautiful trailer while her husband put roofs on the big new houses that were being raised up, all over the county and the city inside it. In places like the Belladonna, where Señora Carmichael lived. Jorge would laugh and say that in America, a man must not be afraid of heights. And once all the boys were in school, Tomasa worked too—for Señor Charley. A rich old man who lived just three trailers away from theirs, who had a son who was not right in the head. A son who was older than she was. But nice. And now her work counted! For seven years she made nearly as much money as Jorge. Tomasa would cook and clean and take care of Charley *pequeño* whenever his father had to go to his job. Where he worked, and what he did, he would not say—but the old man had a big white car and plenty of money. He always carried a little computer with him when he dragged his bad legs out the front door, and it would always be with him when he came back. She wondered if he slept with it.

After he died, the Señora Charley that Tomasa had never seen flew in from someplace else, and she laughed at the finest trailer on the whole street. She gave it away to the Goodwill before she sent her son to the someplace, to live near her. Near her, but not with her. Tomasa tried to write Charley *pequeño* a few words at the Idaho address the Señora Charley left with the mail carrier, but the letters always came back with the same black stamp.

UNKNOWN. UNABLE TO FORWARD.

Desaparecido.

But her husband was still working, and her sons had gone into the Army to serve their new country. Tomasa proudly put three blue stars on her front door, to let the whole world know that this was where *Americanos* came from. Tomasa was happy in her own living room, watching all of her favorite *telenovelas* on her new DVD player. And now she was keeping her own home as spotless as the one she had worked in for seven years. Her life was perfect.

Until her Rafael died. Nobody shot him, or stabbed him, or blew him up. It was a sandstorm that caught the helicopter taking him to the war. It was nobody's fault, the Army said. Nobody attacked him. He was an accident serving his country.

At the funeral, Jorge had too much rum and disgraced himself. The next day, Tomasa put candles around a picture of her lost son, in the living room, surrounded by the pictures of her husband's parents, and of her own parents. The table of the dead, with its American flag and its Timex watch and its *mantilla* and its little *flauta* and its rosary. Her other two sons were safely on another table, in another room. She stuck the gold star over one of the blue ones on the front door. Let the Immigration dare to come for her now.

And then, there were no more roofs for her husband. The banks had fallen down and taken all of the new houses with them. The houses with people already inside wanted real *Americanos* on their roofs when they leaked. Her husband had no work, but he just smiled and said things would change. But things did not change. When they could no longer afford the bill for the cable *deportes*, Jorge began watching *telenovelas* with her on the DVD. She started him off with *Los Ricos Tambien Lloran.*

"You were homeless when I found you," he grinned. "Just like Mariana."

She teased him back. "If I could sing like Mariana, I would not have married you."

"And if I were Luis Alberto, I would not make you give up your baby."

How could her own husband be such a fool? On the screen, Mariana was still singing *Aprendi a Llorar*. Learning to Cry. "I lost him anyway," Tomasa said, standing up, turning her back on him to go into her kitchen.

Because they both agreed they could not ask their living sons for money, Jorge put a sign on his truck, and sold it. She couldn't bear to watch him sign the papers. When he came back into their bedroom and put the fat envelope in Tomasa's two hands, she knew it would have to last them a long time. With no truck, he would have only the work he could find in the trailer park. So the next day she swallowed her pride and walked to the Food Kitchen. There she met Señora Willis, a nice old lady who listened to her story and gave her bags of rice and beans and cans of soup—as much as she could carry home with both arms. The following Wednesday, Señora Willis and her husband drove her—in their own car—to Señora Carmichael, who was not quite so nice but who needed somebody to clean her house, which was big as a church. She would pay her not so much as Señor Charley did, but she would pay her enough. More than enough.

§

SEÑOR CARMICHAEL WAS a rich man whose job was to get money from men who were even richer than he was. He used to play what the *Americanos* call *fútbol*—where they do nothing with their feet except run with them to hit each other. Now he was Vice President of his college. Every Friday during the fall he would have a party for the rich men and their wives—women with faces more like daughters than like wives, but who dressed like *putas*, and who spoke like *putas* after they'd had a few drinks. Tomasa didn't serve them—the students from the college took care of that—but she would hear their filthy words from the kitchen, where she would take out the clean white plates and put their dirty ones into the dishwasher. To catch the last bus home, she would leave before the party was over. Then, the next day, while Señor and Señora Carmichael were at the big *juego*, she would come back to finish her work. To make their big house decent again.

§

THE FIRST THING SHE had to do was gather all of the filthy glasses, which were scattered everywhere. She didn't dare carry more than one at a time. Each felt heavy in her hands, with intricate facets that shone like diamonds. She put them on the dining room table, where they waited for her to take the clean plates from the dishwasher and pile them back in the cupboards.

She didn't see the cat until she came back into the dining room. Somehow it had jumped onto the huge table, filling the only bare space big enough to hold it. Tomasa felt her legs stiffen beneath her. Its stubby white tail was touching at least five glasses. She knew if she moved any closer, *it* would move—and it would break them all.

It was glaring at her, as if it understood her predicament. As if it enjoyed it. It arched its neck and yawned, extending its pink tongue fully, and then lowered itself into a powerful crouch. Tomasa couldn't bear to look. She closed her eyes, and she felt her lips forming a silent prayer. Then she heard a sound like a small bag of corn being thrown into the back of a wagon.

When she opened her eyes, the cat was gone, and every glass was still in a single piece. Before it could come back to try again, she loaded all of them into the dishwasher and selected the proper setting, the one Señora Carmichael had told her to use, so they wouldn't scratch.

A mournful *maullido* came from the living room.

Tomasa had never heard Whitsie make a sound from the mouth before. She had thought the cat was mute. If something happened to it, Señora Carmichael would never forgive her.

She ran into the giant room and saw Whitsie standing on the raised hearth, next to a glass smeared with lipstick from one of the *putas*, who must have been too drunk to put it back on a table. The cat met her eyes, and squinted—and swatted the slender stem as if it were Tomasa's own disapproving finger. She watched the glass turn itself over in the air before shattering against the gray stones.

The cat had stopped looking at her, and had moved on to licking its private parts. It continued its disrespect while Tomasa found a dustpan and swept up every sliver and shard.

"You are an evil *gato*," she muttered. "*Gato malo*."

But it was only one glass, among so many. She would put all the pieces into a plastic bag, and she would throw them away in her own home. How would Señora Carmichael notice?

§

On Monday, Señora Carmichael's exercise class had been cancelled, so she decided to stay home and watch Tomasa work. The giant woman, with limbs as slender and strong as a horse's legs, followed her from room to room—nodding with approval, occasionally straightening a painting on a wall, or adjusting a vase or a diploma or a Certificate of Appreciation on a bookshelf. To Tomasa's annoyance, the cat spent the whole morning in the guest room, sleeping like an angel, never showing the Señora how it truly behaved. How it tripled the work. "You're slow, but thorough," she said, while Tomasa was putting her coat back on in the foyer. "I like that."

"Thank you, Señora Carmichael."

"I'm so happy Hilda Willis found you. And brought you here. But before you leave today, is there something you'd like to tell me? As one Christian to another?"

Tomasa already had her hand on the doorknob, and she shook her head.

"Then is there something you *wouldn't* like to tell me?"

She turned around, with her head lowered, and then looked up to see Whitsie in the woman's arms.

"I want you to be honest with me, Tomasa."

So she told the Señora about her evil *gato*. How it made her vacuum each room again and again, how it jumped on the dining room table, how it mocked her, how it broke the heavy glass in the living room on purpose—to make her lose her job. How she took the pieces home, to hide them, so the Señora would not see.

"Whitsie has never jumped on a table." She put the cat down on the tile floor, and she straightened the plain gold cross around her neck. "Why did you take the glass?"

"I take only the pieces. I can bring them tomorrow, to show you."

"Yes," the woman sighed. "After you break the glass. Just tell me the truth, Tomasa. Nothing will happen to you."

"I tell the truth."

"This is a serious matter, Tomasa." The Señora hadn't let go of her gold chain, and now her bony hand was trembling. "I'll need to pray about this."

Tomasa couldn't stop herself. She reached under her coat and took out her own cross, a real cross, with a real man on it. "Pray for your *gato*, Señora. Not for me."

§

THE NEXT MORNING, Señora Carmichael sat her down at the table in the kitchen. Tomasa felt like a child, in the Señor's big chair that didn't even let her feet touch the floor. She stared at her own hands while she waited for the Señora to speak.

"Haven't we been good enough to you, Tomasa? Do you need more money?"

She told the Señora that everyone needed more money, but yes, the Señora had been good. "And I have been good, too." When she looked up, she saw that the Señora's jaw was already full of what she was going to say next.

"Here's what I've decided. If you tell me the truth, Tomasa, you can stay. And you don't have to pay for the glass. But if you keep lying . . . ." The Señora kept talking about honesty and faith and integrity and responsibility. Responsibility. About the key to the front door Tomasa had been entrusted with.

What could she do? Ever since Señor Charley die and his son go away with his mother, she had no work. Her husband had no work. She looked at her hands again, as if in shame. "I break the glass."

Señora Carmichael left the room and came back with the cat in her arms. "Now apologize to Whitsie."

After Tomasa had finished, Señora Carmichael smiled for the first time that morning. "There. That wasn't so hard, was it?" And she poured Tomasa some coffee, the strong kind that *Americanos* like, as if *she* were the servant. She talked as if nothing had happened. All the time, the cat stayed with them in the kitchen. When the Señora stood up at eleven o'clock to go to her church, she touched Tomasa gently on her right shoulder and said, "I'll leave the two of you to your work."

In the silent house, she heard the front door open, then relatch. Tomasa poured what was left of the bitter coffee into the sink, and ran the water so it wouldn't make a stain that she would have to clean later. While she was washing the cup by hand with the Liquid Joy, she told herself that the Señora was a good woman. That she was doing only what Tomasa would have done in her own home, with her own children, if her father's *flauta* had been missing from the table of the dead. The Señora was wrong, but she was a good woman. Tomasa fingered her crucifix, and she thought of her own first son. Tears began to form at the corners of her eyes while she imagined the Señora at her church with the empty cross. What good is a cross without a God to suffer with you?

Now Whitsie began rubbing against her leg. "Evil *gato*," she grimaced, pushing it away with the side of her shoe. But the cat jumped onto the kitchen table, next to a vase filled with silk chrysanthemums, and stared. Then, after a full minute, it leaped over the false flowers straight to the tile floor, and trotted downstairs to use the litterbox.

"*Gracias a Dios*," she said aloud. And because she was giving thanks, and because it was November, God gave her an idea.

She walked to the big drawer next to the double ovens and took out the clear plastic tube that they would use with the turkey. Then, because she knew it would not be enough, she found an open package of the long straws the Carmichaels stuck into their big drinks.

They do not count their straws, she thought. But she would wash it anyway, when she was finished, and she would unbend it, and she would put it back with the rest.

She walked into the guest room—Whitsie's favorite room. The Carmichaels never had overnight guests, just the parties, but it had its own plumbing. Tomasa knew enough to run the faucet in the sink once every other week, so the drain trap would not dry out and let the stench from the sewer come up through the pipe. Now she fit the straw on the end of the turkey baster and took up all the water from the trap, and she carried it to the toilet. She had to go back and forth three times, but she did not drop a drop. When she waved her hand over the open drain, she could feel the stink begin to tickle her nose.

The cat had come up from downstairs, and it had settled into its favorite spot on the carpet. "You are early today," she smiled. "I have not yet cleaned." After she went downstairs herself, to clear Whitsie's litterbox, she began her vacuuming in the master bedroom.

§

It took more than a week for the Señora to notice, but it took the cat one day less. When Tomasa arrived on a bright Thursday morning, the two of them were waiting for her in the foyer. She was told take the day off. With full pay. The Señora had already seen Whitsie the evening before, sniffing around the blue carpet at the threshold of the guest bathroom. And she had smelled the smell. The carpet would be torn up and replaced that afternoon, just in time for the *fútbol* party tomorrow night. Now the cat was in a carrier that looked like a prison cell with plastic handles, and the Señora was taking him to the animal shelter. She loved him, but he could no longer be trusted.

"He always use his box before," Tomasa said. "Let me see." While the Señora folded her arms in fury in the guest room, Tomasa knelt to sniff the carpet. She soured her face, stood up, and rinsed her hands in the sink, to refill the drain trap—so the Señora's nose would notice the difference later that day, after the workmen left.

Back in the foyer, they were both staring at the white cat in its shiny cage. "You were right, Tomasa. I should have listened to you."

Tomasa asked what would happen at the shelter.

"A ten-year-old cat who can't be trusted? The girl on the phone told me they can't even place half the kittens that come in. I don't think anyone will take him. But he can't stay here."

What had she done? What could she do? "Then I will take him," Tomasa finally said, her shame turning into something even darker as she kept speaking. "My house is not so perfect." She picked up the carrier and whispered, "I bring back the cage tomorrow."

§

GATO

JORGE LOVED THE *gato*. He had never had one before. While Tomasa was at work, it would keep him company, watching the *telenovelas* with him, curled in his lap. He stroked the back of its neck with a tenderness that Tomasa remembered but that she herself had not felt in more than a few years. Her jealousy bristled the hair of her own neck. And because the *gato* cost them nothing, she could not complain. If she did, she would sound like a fool. Her husband fed it from his own plate, and he took care of its box every day, filling it with fresh sand from the Highway Department across the road. They let him have it for free.

One cold night in January, when she turned in her sleep, she opened her eyes to see two yellow *ojos*, full of the moonlight between her own face and her husband's heavy breathing. *Gato malo*. She hissed, but it would not blink. And her heart knew that she would have to do something again.

§

THE NEXT MORNING in Belladonna, after Señora Carmichael left for her shopping, Tomasa took out the turkey baster and the long straw for the second time. She drained the elbow beneath the guest room sink, and she went about her daily work. A few hours later, she brought the Señora back to the room before she even had time to put down her purse.

"It was the sink," Tomasa said, waving her hand above the open stopper. "We no use it enough." Now she opened the spigot fully, and waved her hand again. "The smell go away."

The Señora dropped her purse to the bathroom floor.

"No *gato malo*," Tomasa lied. She would tell the Señora only the sharpest piece of the truth. "Whitsie always use the box in my house."

"I miss him." Now it was the Señora's turn to cry, in huge, wracking sobs nearly as big as she was. "I miss him so much, Tomasa."

Los Ricos Tambien Lloran. "I will ask my husband," Tomasa said, forcing the corners of her own mouth to stay pointed at the marble floor. "But I think he say no."

§

JORGE DID SAY NO, despite all of Tomasa's pleading. He would not give up his *gato*, the *gato* he loved, for the *gringa* who gave him away in the first place. Who would have let him die for the sake of her carpet, which he did not even ruin. He had seen such women from up on his roofs, when he still had roofs, in places like the Belladonna—treating their children like animals, and treating their animals like dirt one minute and like *Dios* the next. "Tell her I do not trust her," he said. "That she does not deserve this *gato*."

And so, the next day, she did.

§

THERE WERE NO MORE *juegos* on Saturday afternoons at the college, so Tomasa did not have an extra day of work. She was watching her newest *telenovela* with Jorge and the *gato*, when the doorbell rang. When she pulled back her curtains to look, she saw a car so shiny that it hurt her eyes, standing in the place where her husband used to park his truck, when he had a truck. Señora and Señor Carmichael had both come to their trailer—how had they found it, among so many others?—to see Whitsie.

"I apologize," Señor Carmichael said, looking away from his wife. "She insisted we speak with you in person."

"*De nada*," Jorge said. He muted the sound on the *telenovela*, but he did not turn it off. Then, to Tomasa's amazement, he stood up from his recliner and handed the *gato* to the big man, who handed it to his wife. The Señora's eyes glowed until the cat wriggled free, and jumped back into Jorge's lap.

"Seems like you've got a friend there," the big man grinned. "A real amigo."

Now Señora Carmichael turned her thin shoulders, so she could hide her broken face from all of them. To give her shame something to do, the big woman began studying the *fotografías* on the table of the dead. She put out her hand, as if to touch each one, but she did not touch. Jorge's father. His mother. Her father. Her mother. The boy in the uniform, surrounded by candles.

"My son," Tomasa said.

"Our son," Jorge said, shaping his hands to the cat's body as he stroked it on both sides at once.

"We never had children," the Señora said, still weeping. "I can only imagine."

You can never imagine, Tomasa thought. *But now you can try.*

"I put the roof over your house," Jorge said to the man. "In the Belladonna."

"It's a good roof," the man said.

"The roofs miss him," Tomasa said. "They miss him very much."

For five minutes, they all watched the silent figures on the screen—as if more than words were hidden in the mouths of the beautiful *hombres* and the beautiful *mujeres* that no one could hear. When Tomasa could stand it no longer, she took the remote control from her husband's hand, and she turned the television into an empty box. Still no one spoke. Then she picked up her mother's own rosary, walked three heavy steps to the Señora, and asked her if she wanted to pray.

Acknowledgments

The author wishes to thank the editors of the following publications, in which some of the work in this volume appeared in earlier forms: *Brutarian* ("Hospital Food"); *China Grove* ("Treenapping"); *Eclectica* ("The Eye of the Needle"); *Emrys Journal* ("Fat Eyes"); *The Evansville Review* ("Gato"); *Kestrel* ("Standard Kung Fu Mayhem"); *Peeks & Valleys* ("Nobody Ever Looked Back on Life and Wished for a Station Wagon"); *Southeast Review* ("Inflatable Kids"); *The Southern Review* ("Trash"); *The State* ("Prayers"); *Tampa Review* ("Dog Days"); *undefined magazine* ("Weather").

He also thanks *Pushcart Prize XXXVII* (which awarded a Special Mention to "Trash"), the Charlotte Writers Club (which awarded the Elizabeth Simpson Smith Prize to "Trash"), *The Cantabrigian Magazine* (for reprinting "Trash" in its 2018 issue), *Food and Other Enemies: Stories of Consuming Desire* (for reprinting "Fat Eyes"), the Porter Fleming Foundation (which awarded prizes to "Hospital Food" and "The Eye of the Needle"), and the South Carolina Arts Commission (which awarded the South Carolina Fiction Prize to "Prayers") for their encouragement and support.

This book was set in Sabon, designed by the German typographer and book designer, Jan Tschichold, and released in 1967. Tschichold was inspired to design Sabon after encountering a sixteenth-century specimen sheet produced by the legendary printer and typographer, Claude Garamond (1480–1561). The typeface is named after one of Garamond's students and colleagues, Jacques Sabon (1535–ca. 1580–90).

This book was designed by Shannon Carter, Ian Creeger, and Gregory Wolfe. It was published in hardcover, paperback, and electronic formats by Wipf and Stock Publishers, Eugene, Oregon.